# The
# Eighteen-carat Kid
## *and Other Stories*

# The
# Eighteen-carat Kid
## and Other Stories by
# P. G. Wodehouse

### Edited and Introduced by
## DAVID A. JASEN

CONTINUUM / New York

1980
The Continuum Publishing Corporation
815 Second Avenue, New York, N.Y. 10017

Introduction copyright © 1980 by David A. Jasen.
No part of this book may be reproduced, stored in
a retrieval system, or transmitted, in any form
or by any means, electronic, mechanical, photocopying,
recording, or otherwise, without the written
permission of The Continuum Publishing Corporation.
*Printed in the United States of America*
*Designed by Victoria Gomez*

Library of Congress Cataloging in Publication Data

Wodehouse, Pelham Grenville, 1881–1975.
The eighteen-carat kid, and other stories.
    I. Jasen, David A.   II. Title.
PZ3.W817Ei    [PR6045.053]    823′.912    80-14012
            ISBN 0-8264-0012-4

# Contents

To Julian Mates,
whose own love of PGW may
have contributed to the reason
that he is the nicest boss
I have ever had.

# Introduction
# by David A. Jasen

P. G. Wodehouse, as has been said, was the foremost humorist of the twentieth century. The word *humorist* was chosen wisely, to indicate cheerfulness, happiness, exhilaration, exuberance, geniality, lightheartedness, and liveliness—all qualities with which Wodehouse's writings are filled.

He was a comic writer whose main source of income was derived from sales to magazines in England and in the United States. After 1920 the greater part of his writings first appeared in periodicals and then were put between hard covers and sold as books in both countries. In recent years, translations have appeared in over one hundred countries and his popularity has remained high the world over. Originally, "The Eighteen-carat Kid" appeared as a serial in the very popular English magazine "for boys and Old Boys," *The Captain*. The following story, "The Wire-Pullers," appeared in *The Strand*, England's greatest mass magazine for the middle-classes, comparable to our old *Saturday Evening Post*, to which Plum also contributed with great success. "The Prize Poem" came from *The Public School Magazine*, which was published by A. & C. Black, which also issued *William Tell Told Again* as a book.

Today, in the United States, television has usurped the function of the general mass magazine and would-be comic writers are writing situation comedies for television instead of humorous short stories and novels. Unfortunately, there is no place in our society today for the comic writer of prose.

When Wodehouse was starting out at the turn of this century in London, there were newspapers and plenty of magazines of general interest which would accept his humorous articles, essays, poems, short stories, and serials. He wrote, it seems, for practically all of them. We are now making available the best of his early writings—for the first time in the United States.

Atmosphere was what separated the good comic writers from the bad. Wodehouse was particularly adept at establishing his atmosphere and maintaining it throughout at a consistently high level. Although he worried for the rest of his considerable life (he was born on 15 October 1881 and died on 14 February 1975) about his plots (they were nearly all the same), it was the way he expressed himself—his use of the English language—mixing formal with slang to produce hilariously unexpected results, which gave his reading public its extreme delight.

His was the humor (very rare indeed) of geniality, of kindheartedness. He did not achieve a laugh at the expense of a character, nor as today's stand-up comics do by getting a cheap laugh merely by mentioning a familiar (but not in itself funny) name or experience. Nor did he denigrate or put anyone up to ridicule. Many earlier critics made the mistake of calling Plum a satirist, but there was hardly anything about which he was being satirical. No, he stood alone for most of his professional life (1900–1975) as a consistently reliable humorist. And, the public responded appropriately. He was the only comic writer constantly in demand over several decades. He received the largest sums of money for his magazine efforts. The Wodehouse name on the cover meant a substantial increase in that issue's sales. Not only was he in great demand by both magazine editors and readers, but his broad appeal spanned nearly four full generations.

The Wodehouse world was one of his own creation, peopled not with beings from the real world, but from his own imagination. His popularity was gained not by caricaturing the real world or by holding up a mirror, but by taking universal traits and easily recognizable habits and making us see ourselves through his make-believe people in perfectly constructed, yet enormously complicated make-believe situations.

*The Eighteen-carat Kid,* originally published in 1913, is set in a preparatory school isolated on spacious grounds two miles from the nearest town. During this time in Plum's career he would take places and people from real life and use them in his stories. A few years earlier, he had been invited to stay at Emsworth House where his friend Herbert Westbook (see *Not George Washington,* Continuum) was an assistant master. He took rooms above the stable where he wrote in comparative solitude (notice the description of the thickness of the walls). Later, he rented a cottage called "Threepwood" in the village of Emsworth, down the road from the school (alluded to in passing). There was plenty of chance to study the school environment and the reaction of the boys. His two earlier visits to the United States (the first in 1904, the second in 1909) gave him the opportunity to hear the talk of American toughs (he hung around training camps for boxers and lived for a while in Greenwich Village), all of which is reflected in this serial.

In the United States during the early part of the second decade of this century, divorce was an increasingly discussed topic—used more for its shock value in literature and on the stage than for any real offer of help. In a rare awareness and literary use of social problems, Plum solved his divorce situation by offering very practical advice, which is taken at story's end.

In keeping with his essential kindliness and gentleness,

Plum endows even his crooks with pleasing characteristics. From the beginning the reader has a warm feeling for Smooth Sam which is maintained until the end.

With the publication of "The Wire-Pullers" in the July, 1905 issue of *The Strand,* Plum began a remarkable thirty-five-year association with England's premiere general magazine for the literate. The subject matter and treatment of cricket, a favorite sport of Plum's, was not so very far removed from his schoolboys' stories. Writing about what he knew and liked worked well with the young author, as rejection slips became a thing of the past and all of his efforts saw the light of publication.

"The Prize Poem" has the distinction of being the first of Plum's short stories to be published in a magazine. An earlier short story, "When Papa Swore in Hindustani" (see *The Uncollected Wodehouse,* Continuum), was published a bit later in a weekly newspaper. *The Public School Magazine,* in which "The Prize Poem" appeared in the issue of July 1901, was started by the publishing firm of Adam & Charles Black three years earlier. Plum's career could be said to have fairly begun with this short story in a regularly published magazine. The early success of *The Public School Magazine* prompted George Newnes Limited to come out with a rival magazine called *The Captain.* Newnes was also publishing *The Strand.* And at the time when A. & C. Black decided to fold *The Public School Magazine,* Plum was firmly established with *The Captain,* while Black began publishing Plum in hard covers.

*William Tell Told Again* was Plum's only children's book. A. & C. Black commissioned him to write it around some sixteen color illustrations they had bought from Philip Dadd as far back as 1900. Plum's retelling of the children's classic was originally published on 11 November 1904. The Epilogue is characteristic of Plum's universality—the message is just as meaningful today as when it was written.

# The
# Eighteen-carat Kid

## Chapter 1
## THE ARRIVAL OF OGDEN

There is always something going on in a private school, but I think I may say that, until the arrival of Ogden Ford, we were, on the whole, a quiet little community at Sanstead House (Arnold Abney, M.A., proprietor). It was my first term at the school. I was one of the two assistant masters, and the place suited me. Beyond breaking up fights, stopping big boys bullying small boys, preventing small boys bullying smaller boys, inducing boys of all sizes not to throw stones, go on the wet grass, worry the cook, tease the cat, make too much noise, climb trees, scale waterspouts, lean too far out of windows, slide down the banisters, swallow pencils, and drink ink because somebody bet them they wouldn't, I had very little to do except teach mathematics, carve the joint, help the pudding, play football, read prayers, herd stragglers into meals, and go round the dormitories at night to see that the lights were out. In fact, until the advent of Ogden my life was practically one of fatted ease.

I liked the spot in which Fate had placed me, Sanstead House, a large building in the Georgian style, standing in the midst of about nine acres of land. For the greater part of its existence it had been the private home of a family of the name of Boone, and in its early days the estate had been considerable. But the progress of the years had brought changes to the Boones. Money losses had necessitated the sale of land. New roads had come into being, cutting off portions of the estate from their center. New facilities for travel had drawn members of the family away from home. The old fixed life of the country had changed, and in the end the latest Boone had come to the conclusion that to keep up such a large and expensive house was not worth his while.

That the place should have become a school was the natural process of evolution. The house was too large for the ordinary purchaser, and the estate had been so whittled down in the course of time, that it was inadequate for the wealthy. Colonel Boone had been glad to let it to Mr. Abney, and the school had started on its career.

It had all the necessary qualifications for a school. It was isolated. The village was two miles from its gates. It was near the sea. There were fields for cricket and football, and inside the house a number of rooms of every size, suitable for classrooms and dormitories.

The household consisted, besides Mr. Abney, myself, another master named Glossop, and the matron, of twenty-four boys, a lady-housekeeper, White the butler, the cook, the odd-job man, two housemaids, a scullery-maid, and a parlor-maid. It was a little colony, cut off from the outer world.

And then, breaking into our peaceful world, came Ogden Ford.

It was a freckled youth of the name of Beckford who first told me of his existence. He always got hold of any piece of gossip first.

"There's a new kid coming tonight, sir!" he said. "An American kid. Mr. Abney's going up to London to fetch him. The kid's name's Ford. I believe the kid's father's awfully rich. Would you like to be rich, sir? I wish I were rich."

He pondered the point a moment. "If you wanted a halfpenny to make up twopence to buy a lizard, what would you do, sir?"

He got it.

Ogden Ford entered Sanstead House at a quarter past nine that evening. He was preceded by a Worried Look, Mr. Arnold Abney, a cabman carrying a large box, and the odd-job man carrying two suitcases. I have given precedence to the "worried look" because it was a thing by itself. To say that Mr. Abney wore it would be to create a wrong impression. Mr. Abney simply followed in its wake. He caught sight of me, and stopped.

"Ah, Mr. Burns, I should like to speak to you. Let us go into the dining room."

Mr. Abney was a tall, suave, benevolent man, with an Oxford manner, a high forehead, thin white hands, a cooing intonation, and a general air of hushed importance. As a rule, he preserved a dignified calm, but now this had temporarily deserted him. He applied a silk handkerchief to his forehead before he spoke.

"That is a boy called Ford, Mr. Burns," he said. "A rather—er—remarkable boy. He is an American, the son of Mr. Elmer Ford, of whom you have possibly heard."

I remembered having seen the name in the papers. "The multimillionaire?"

"Exactly. He struck me as a man of great ability, a typical American merchant-prince. Mr. Ford was singularly frank with me about his domestic affairs, and I am bound to say they explain to a great extent little Ogden's—ah—peculiarities. It seems that until now Mrs. Ford has had sole charge of the boy's upbringing, and—Mr. Ford was singularly outspoken—was too indulgent, in fact—ah—spoilt him. Mr. Ford regards this school as, in a measure—what shall I say?—an antidote. He wishes there to be no lack of wholesome discipline, of which, I am afraid, there is the profoundest need. I am disposed to imagine that Ogden has been, from childhood up, systematically indulged. The result is that, while I have no doubt that *au fond—au fond* he is a charming boy, quite charming, at present he is—shall I say?—peculiar. He has tastes and ideas which are precocious, and unusual in a lad of his age. He expresses himself in a curious manner at times. He seems to have little or no reverence for—ah—constituted authority. He——"

He paused while he passed his handkerchief once more over his forehead.

"He will be a great deal in your care, Mr. Burns. I shall expect you to check firmly, though, of course, kindly, such habits of his as—ah—cigarette-smoking——"

"Does he smoke?"

Mr. Abney looked troubled.

"On our journey down from London he smoked incessantly. I found it impossible, without physical violence, to induce him to stop. But, of course, now that he is actually at the school, and subject to the discipline of the school——"

I saw what he meant. He could not handle the boy, so I must. He had handed the case over to me.

"Perhaps it would be as well if you saw him now, Mr. Burns. You will find him in the study."

He drifted away, and I went to the study to introduce myself.

A cloud of tobacco smoke rising above the back of an easy chair greeted me as I opened the door. Moving into the room, I perceived a pair of shoes resting on the grate. I stepped to the right, and the remainder of the new boy came into view.

He was lying almost at full length in the chair, his eyes fixed in dreamy abstraction upon the ceiling. As I came towards him, he drew at the cigarette between his fingers, glanced at me, looked away again, and expelled another mouthful of smoke. He was not interested in me.

Perhaps this indifference piqued me, and I saw him with prejudiced eyes. At any rate, he seemed to me a singularly unprepossessing youth. His age, I suppose, was about fourteen. He had a stout body and a round, unwholesome face. His eyes were dull, and his mouth drooped discontentedly. He had the air of one who is surfeited with life.

"Throw away that cigarette," I said.

To my amazement he did, promptly. I was beginning to wonder whether I had not been too abrupt—he gave me a curious sensation of being a man of my own age—when he produced a silver case from his pocket, and opened it. I saw that the cigarette in the fender was a stump.

I took the case from his hand, and threw it on to a table. For the first time he seemed really to notice my existence.

"You've got a nerve," he said. "What do you want to come butting in for?"

"I am paid to butt in. It's the main duty of an assistant master."

"Oh, you're the assistant master, are you?"

"One of them. And, in passing—it's a small technical point—you call me 'sir' when you speak to me."

"Call you 'sir!' Up an alley!"

"I beg your pardon?"

"Fade away! Take a walk!"

I gathered that he was meaning to convey that he did not care to entertain my proposition.

"You needn't think you can breeze in here, telling me to do things," he proceeded. "I know all about this joint. The hot-air merchant was telling me about it on the train."

I took the allusion to be to Mr. Arnold Abney.

"He's the boss, and nobody but him is allowed to hit the

fellows. If you tried it, you'd lose your job. And he isn't going to, because dad's paying double fees, and he's scared stiff he'll lose me if there's any trouble."

"You seem to have a grasp of the position."

"Bet your life I have."

It was borne in upon me that I was getting the loser's end of this dialogue. I changed the subject.

"You had better go to bed. It's past your proper time."

He stared at me in open-eyed amazement.

"Bed!"

"Bed."

He seemed more amused than annoyed.

"Say, what time do you think I usually go to bed?"

"I know what time you go here. Nine o'clock."

As if to support my words, the door opened, and Mrs. Attwell, the matron, entered.

"I think it's time he came to bed, Mr. Burns."

"I was just suggesting it, Mrs. Attwell."

"You're crazy," observed the little nugget.

Mrs. Attwell looked at me despairingly.

"I never saw such a boy!"

The whole machinery of the school was being held up by this legal infant. Any vacillation now, and Authority would suffer a setback from which it would be hard put to it to recover. It seemed to me a situation that called for action.

I bent down, scooped him out of his chair like an oyster, and made for the door.

He yelled incessantly. Outside he kicked me in the stomach, and then on the knee. He continued to scream. He screamed all the way upstairs, and he was screaming when we reached his room.

## Chapter 2
# THINGS BEGIN TO HAPPEN

It was the custom at Sanstead House for each of the assistant masters to take half of one day in every week as a holiday. The allowance was not liberal, and in most schools, I believe, it is increased; but Mr. Abney was a man with peculiar views on other people's holidays, and Glossop and I were accordingly restricted.

My day was Wednesday; and on the Wednesday following the arrival of Ogden Ford I left the house and strolled to the village for a game of billiards at the local inn.

Sanstead House and its neighborhood were lacking in the fiercer metropolitan excitements, and billiards at the "Feathers" constituted for the pleasure-seeker the beginning and end of the Gay Whirl.

There was a local etiquette governing the game of billiards at the "Feathers." You played the marker a hundred up, then you took him into the bar-parlor and bought him refreshment. After that, you could, if you wished, play another game, or go home, as your fancy dictated.

There was only one other occupant of the bar-parlor when we adjourned thither. He was lying back in a chair, with his feet on the side table, apparently wrapped in thought.

He was a short, tough, clean-shaven man, with a broken nose, over which was tilted a soft felt hat. His wiry limbs were clad in a ready-made tweed suit. He was smoking a peculiarly evil-smelling cigar.

We had hardly seated ourselves when he rose and lurched out.

"American!" said Miss Benjafield, the stately barmaid, with strong disapproval.

I breathed sympathetically.

"What he's here for I'd like to know," said Miss Benjafield. "No good, if you ask me."

She seemed to feel quite strongly on the subject.

It was not late when I started on my way back to the House, but the short January day was over, and it was very dark as I turned in at the big gate of the school and made my way up the drive. The drive at Sanstead House was a fine curving stretch of gravel, about two hundred yards in length, flanked on either side by fir trees and rhododendrons. I stepped out briskly, for it had begun to freeze. Just as I caught sight through the trees of the lights of the windows, there came to me the sound of running feet.

I stopped. The noise grew louder. There seemed to be two runners, one moving with short, quick steps, the other— the one in front—taking a longer stride.

I drew aside instinctively. In another moment, making a great clatter on the frozen gravel, the first of the pair passed me, and as he did so there was a sharp crack, and something sang through the darkness like a large mosquito.

The effect of the sound on the man who had been running was immediate. He stopped in his stride, and dived into the bushes. His footsteps thudded faintly on the turf.

The whole incident had lasted only a few seconds, and I was still standing there, when I was aware of the other man approaching. He had apparently given up the pursuit, for he was walking quite slowly. He stopped within a few feet of me, and I heard him swearing softly to himself.

"Who's that?" I cried, sharply. The crack of the pistol had given a flick to my nerves. Mine had been a sheltered life, into which hitherto revolver shots had not entered, and I was resenting this abrupt introduction of them. I felt jumpy and irritated.

It gave me a malicious pleasure to see that I had startled the unknown dispenser of shocks quite as much as he had startled me. The movement he made as he faced round in my direction was almost a leap; and it suddenly flashed upon me that I had better at once establish my identity as a non-combatant. I appeared to have wandered inadvertently into the midst of a private quarrel, one party to which—the one standing a couple of yards from me with a loaded revolver in his hand—was evidently a man of impulse—the sort of man who would shoot first and inquire afterwards.

"I'm Mr. Burns," I said. "I'm one of the assistant masters. Who are you?"

"Mr. Burns!"

Surely that rich voice was familiar.

"White?" I said.

"Yes, sir."

White, the butler, was rather a friend of mine. He was a stout, but active man of middle age. We had established pleasant relations on my first evening in the place, when he had helped me unpack my box. He lacked that quality of austere aloofness which I have noticed in other butlers. There was a geniality about him that I liked. He was new to Sanstead, like myself. His predecessor had left at short notice during the holidays.

"What on earth are you doing, White?" I said. "Who was that man?"

"I wish I knew, sir. I found him prowling at the back of the house very suspicious. He took to his heels and I followed him."

"But——" I spoke querulously. My orderly nature was shocked. "You can't go shooting at people like that just because you find them at the back of the house. What were you doing with a revolver?"

"I secured it from the man in the struggle."

"Struggle?"

"When he saw me he drew the revolver, and I grappled with him."

I became excited. "We must 'phone to the police station. Could you describe the man?"

"I think not, sir. It was very dark. And, if I may make the

suggestion, it would be better not to inform the police. I have a very poor opinion of these country constables."

"But we can't have men prowling——"

"If you will permit me, sir, I say—let them prowl. It's the only way to catch them."

"If you think this sort of thing is likely to happen again, I must tell Mr. Abney."

"Pardon me, sir, I think it would be better not. He impresses me as a somewhat nervous gentleman, and it would only disturb him. May I ask you to respect my confidence, sir, if I tell you something? I came here anticipating something of this kind. In fact, I was sent here for the purpose of guarding against it. I'm a private inquiry agent, Mr. Burns. A detective."

"A detective!"

"Mr. Elmer Ford sent me here to look after his son. There are several parties after that boy, Mr. Burns. Kidnappers. He's Mr. Ford's only son, so naturally he is a considerable prize. Mr. Ford would pay a large sum to get him back if he were kidnapped. Over in America there have been several attempts to get him. Buck Macginnis tried it twice. So did Chicago Ed. Smooth Sam Fisher had one go, and came nearest to getting away with him of them all. You take it from me, sir, that it's Smooth Sam who's going to bring it off if anybody does. Buck's just a common Bowery tough, but Sam's a man of education. He's a college man, Sam is. And I happen to know he's on the trail. So's Buck for that matter. Old man Ford got that kid out of America pretty quietly, but not quietly enough. Sam and Buck are both here, trailing him. Not that Buck counts," he added, contemptuously, "I don't give a flip for Buck. Sam's got brains."

"Does Mr. Abney know you are a detective?"

"No, sir. Mr. Abney thinks I am an ordinary butler. You are the only person who knows, and I have only told you because you have happened to catch me in a rather queer

position for a butler to be in. You will keep it to yourself, sir?
It doesn't do for it to get about. These things have to be
done quietly. It would be bad for the school if my presence
here were advertised. The other parents wouldn't like it.
They would think that their sons were in danger, you see. It
would be disturbing for them. So if you will just forget what
I've been telling you, Mr. Burns——"

I assured him that I would. But I did not think it likely.
One may forget a good many things in this world, but
disguised detectives, Buck Macginnises, and Smooth Sam
Fishers are, as far as I am concerned, not among them.

## *Chapter 3*
# OGDEN LOSES HIS BEAUTY SLEEP

I owed it to my colleague Glossop that I was in the center of
the surprising things that occurred that night. Glossop was
not an entertaining companion. By sheer weight of boredom
he drove me from the house, so that it came about that, at
half-past nine, the time at which the affair began, I was pa-
trolling the gravel in front of the porch.

It was the practice of the staff of Sanstead House School
to assemble after dinner in Mr. Abney's study for coffee.
The room was called the "Study," but it was really more of a
masters' common-room. Mr. Abney had a smaller sanctum
of his own, reserved exclusively for himself. To this he
would sometimes depart of a night in order to write letters.

On this particular night he went there early, leaving me
alone with Glossop. And after ten minutes of Glossop I decided for solitude.

Except for my bedroom, whither he was quite capable of

following me, I had no refuge but the grounds. I unbolted the front door and went out.

It was still freezing, and, though the stars shone, the trees grew so closely about the house that it was too dark for me to see more than a few feet in front of me.

I began to stroll up and down. The night was wonderfully still. I could even hear a bird rustling in the ivy on the wall of the stables.

I had reached the end of my "beat," and had stopped to relight my pipe, when the stillness of the night was split by a sound which I could have heard in a gale and recognized among a hundred conflicting noises. It was a scream, a shrill, piercing squeal that did not rise to a crescendo, but started at its maximum and held the note; a squeal which could only proceed from one throat; the deafening war cry of Ogden Ford.

It cannot have been more than a few seconds later before some person unknown nearly destroyed me. Rounding the angle of the house in a desperate hurry, he emerged from the bushes, and rammed me squarely.

He was a short man, or he must have crouched as he ran, for his shoulder, a hard, bony shoulder, was precisely the same distance from the ground as my solar plexus. In the brief impact which ensued between the two, the shoulder had the advantage of being in motion, while the solar plexus was stationary, and there was no room for any shadow of doubt as to which had the worst of it.

That the mysterious unknown was not unshaken by the encounter was made clear by a sharp yelp of surprise and pain. He staggered. What happened to him after that was not a matter of interest to me. I gather that he escaped into the night. But I was too occupied with my own affairs to follow his movements. I can remember reeling across the gravel and falling in a heap and trying to breathe, and knowing that I should never again be able to, and then for some minutes all interest in the affairs of this world left me.

When I had leisure to observe outside matters I perceived that among the other actors in the drama confusion still reigned. There was much scuttering about, and much meaningless shouting. Mr. Abney's voice was issuing directions, each of which seemed more futile than the last. Glossop was repeating over and over again the words, "Shall I telephone for the police?" One or two boys were darting about like rabbits and squealing unintelligibly. A female voice—I think, Mrs. Attwell's—was saying, "Can you see him?"

Somebody, who proved to be White, the butler, came from the direction of the stable yard with a carriage lamp. Everyone seemed calmer and happier for it.

The whole strength of the company gathered round the light.

"Thank you, White," said Mr. Abney. "Excellent. I fear the scoundrel has escaped."

"I suspect so, sir."

"This is a very remarkable occurrence, White."

"Undeniably singular, sir."

"The man was actually in Master Ford's bedroom."

"Indeed, sir?"

A shrill voice spoke. I recognised it as that of the boy Beckford, always to be counted upon to be in the center of things, gathering information.

"Sir, please, sir, what was up? Who was it, sir? Sir, was it a burglar, sir? Have you ever met a burglar, sir? My father took me to see *Raffles* in the holidays, sir. Do you think this chap was like Raffles, sir? Sir——"

"It was undoubtedly——" Mr. Abney was beginning, when the identity of the questioner dawned upon him, and for the first time he realized that the drive was full of boys actively engaged in catching their deaths of cold. His all-friends-here-let-us-discuss-this-interesting-episode-fully manner changed. He became the outraged schoolmaster. Never before had I heard him speak so sharply to boys, many of whom, though breaking rules, were still titled.

"What are you boys doing out of bed? Go back to bed instantly. I shall punish you most severely. I——"

"Shall I telephone for the police?" asked Glossop.

"I will not have this conduct! You will catch cold! This is disgraceful! Ten bad marks! I shall punish you most severely if you do not instantly——"

A calm voice interrupted him.

"Say!"

Ogden Ford strolled easily into the circle of light. He was wearing a dressing gown, and in his hand was a smoldering cigarette, from which he proceeded, before continuing his remarks, to blow a cloud of smoke.

"Say, I guess you're wrong. That wasn't any ordinary porch-climber."

The spectacle of his *bête noire* wreathed in smoke, coming on top of the emotions of the night, was almost too much for Mr. Abney. He gesticulated for a moment in impassioned silence, his arms throwing grotesque shadows on the gravel.

"How *dare* you smoke, boy? How *dare* you smoke that cigarette?"

"It's the only one I've got," responded Ogden, amiably.

"I have spoken to you—I have warned you—Ten bad marks! I will not have——Fifteen bad marks!"

Ogden ignored the painful scene. He was smiling, quietly.

"If you ask *me*," he said, "that guy was after something better than plated spoons. Yes, sir! If you want my opinion, it was Buck Macginnis, or Smooth Sam Fisher, or one of those guys, and what he was trailing was me. They're always at it. Buck had a try for me in the Fall of '07, and Sam——"

"Do you hear me? Will you return instantly——"

"If you don't believe me, I can show you the piece there was about it in the papers. I've got a press-clipping album in my box. Whenever there's a piece about me in the papers I

cut it out and paste it into my album. If you'll come right
along, I'll show you the story about Buck now. It happened
in Chicago, and he'd have got away with me if it hadn't
been——"

"Twenty bad marks!"

"Mr. Abney," I said.

They jumped, all together, like a well-trained chorus.

"Who is that?" cried Mr. Abney. I could tell by the sound
of his voice that his nerves were on wires. "Who was that
who spoke?"

"Shall I telephone for the police?" asked Glossop. (Ignored.)

They made for me in a body, boys and all, White leading
with the lantern. I was almost sorry for being compelled to
provide an anticlimax.

"Mr. Burns! What—dear me!—*what* are you doing there?"
said Mr. Abney.

"Perhaps Mr. Burns can give us some information as to
where the man went, sir," suggested White.

"On everything except that," I said, "I'm a mine of information. I haven't the least idea where he went. All I know
about him is that he has a shoulder like the ram of a battle-
ship, and that he charged me with it. I was strolling about
when I heard a scream——" A chuckle came from the group
behind the lantern.

"*I* screamed," said Ogden. "You bet I screamed. What
would *you* do if you woke up in the dark and found a strong-
armed roughneck prising you out of bed as if you were a
clam? He tried to get his hand over my mouth, but he only
connected with my forehead, and I'd got going before he
could switch. I guess I threw a scare into that gink!"

He chuckled again, reminiscently, and drew at his cigarette.

"How dare you smoke! Throw away that cigarette!" cried
Mr. Abney, roused afresh by the red glow.

"Forget it!" advised Ogden tersely.

"And then," I said, "somebody whizzed out from nowhere and hit me. And after that I didn't seem to care much about him or anything else."

I heard Glossop speak, and gathered from Mr. Abney's reply that he had made his suggestion once more. Mr. Abney, like White, believed in keeping things quiet.

"I think that will be—ah—unnecessary, Mr. Glossop. The man has undoubtedly—ah—made good his escape. I think we had all better return to the house."

## *Chapter 4*
# BUCK MACGINNIS

I have never kept a diary, and I find it, in consequence, somewhat difficult, in telling this story, to assign events to their correct times. But I think it was two nights after the happenings related in the last chapter that my meeting with Buck Macginnis took place.

I had fallen into the habit, now that the frost made the ground too hard for football, of taking my daily exercise in the shape of a walk to the village and back after dinner.

On this night I was midway between house and village, when I became aware that I was being followed. The night was dark, and the wind, moving in the treetops, emphasized the loneliness of the country road. Both time and place were such as made it peculiarly unpleasant to hear stealthy footsteps on the road behind me.

Uncertainty in such cases is the unnerving thing. I turned sharply, and began to walk back on tip-toe in the direction from which I had come.

I had not been mistaken. A moment later a dark figure

loomed up out of the darkness, and the exclamation which greeted me, as I made my presence known, showed that I had taken him by surprise.

There was a momentary pause. I expected the man, whoever he might be, to run, but he held his ground. Indeed, he edged forward.

"Get back," I said, and allowed my stick to rasp suggestively on the road, before raising it in readiness for any sudden development. It was as well that he should know it was there.

The hint seemed to wound rather than frighten him.

"Aw, cut out the rough stuff, bo," he said, reproachfully, in a cautious, husky undertone. "I ain't goin' to start anything."

"What are you following me for?" I demanded. "Who are you?"

"Say, I want a talk wit youse. I took a slant at youse under de lamppost back dere, an' I seen it was you, so I tagged along. Say, I'm wise to your game, sport."

I had no notion what he might mean. I had identified him by this time. Unless there were two men in the neighborhood of Sanstead who hailed from America, this must be the man whom I had seen at the "Feathers," who had incurred the disapproval of Miss Benjafield.

"I haven't the faintest idea what you mean," I said. "What is my game?"

His voice became reproachful again.

"Ah, quit yer kiddin'!" he protested. "What was youse rubberin' around de house for dat night, if you wasn't trailin' de kid?"

"That night? Was it you who ran into me?"

"Gee! I t'ought it was a tree. Say, dat's a great kid, dat. We gotta get together about dat kid."

"Certainly, if you wish it. What do you happen to mean?"

"Aw, quit yer kiddin'!" He expectorated again. He seemed

to be a man who could express the whole gamut of emotions by this simple means. "I know you!"

"Then you have the advantage of me. Though I believe I remember seeing you before. Weren't you at the 'Feathers' one Wednesday evening?"

"Sure. Dat was me."

"What do you mean by saying that you know me?"

"Aw, quit yer kiddin', Sam!"

There was, it seemed to me, a reluctantly admiring note in his voice.

"Tell me, who do you think I am?" I asked, patiently.

"Ah! you can't string me, sport! Smooth Sam Fisher is who you are, bo. I know you."

I was too surprised to speak. Verily, some have greatness thrust upon them.

"I hain't never seen youse, Sam," he continued, "but I know it's you. And I'll tell youse how I doped it out. To begin with, there ain't but you and your bunch and me and my bunch dat knows de Ford kid's on dis side at all. Dey sneaked him out of New York mighty slick, and I heard that you had come here after him. So when I runs into a guy dat's trailin' de kid down here, well, who's it going to be if it ain't youse? And when dat guy talks like a dude, like they all say you do, well, who's it going to be if it ain't youse? So quit yer kiddin', Sam, and let's get down to business."

"Have I the pleasure of addressing Mr. Buck Macginnis?" I said. I felt convinced that this could be no other than that celebrity.

"Dat's right. Dere's no need to keep up anyt'ing wit me, Sam. We're bote on de same trail, so let's get down to it."

"One moment," I said. "Would it surprise you to hear that my name is Burns, and that I am a master at the school?"

He chuckled admiringly.

"Sure, no!" he said. "It's just what you would be, Sam. I always heard youse had been one of dese college boys oncest. Say, it's mighty smart of youse to be a professor. You're right in on de ground floor."

His voice became appealing.

"Say, Sam, don't be a hawg. Let's go fifty-fifty on dis deal. Dere's plenty for all of us. Old man Ford'll cough up enough for everyone, and dere won't be any fuss. Let's sit in together, Sam."

As I said nothing, he proceeded.

"It ain't square, Sam, to take advantage of your having education. If it was a square fight, and us both wit de same chance, I wouldn't say; but you bein' a dude professor and gettin right into de job like dat ain't right. Say, don't swipe it all, Sam. Fifty-fifty! Does dat go?"

"I don't know," I said. "You had better ask the real Sam. Good night."

I walked past him, and made for the school gates at my best pace. He trotted after me pleading.

"Sam! Give us a quarter, then."

I walked on.

"Sam! don't be a hawg!"

He broke into a run.

"Sam!"

His voice lost its pleading tone, and rasped menacingly.

"Gum, if I had me canister, youse wouldn't be so flip! Listen here, you big cheese! You t'ink youse is de only t'ing in sight, huh? Well, we ain't done yet. You'll see yet. We'll fix you! Youse had best watch out."

I stopped, and turned on him.

"Look here, you fool," I cried, "I tell you I am not Sam Fisher. Can't you understand that you have got hold of the wrong man? My name is Burns—*Burns.*"

He was a man slow by nature to receive ideas, but slower to rid himself of one that had contrived to force its way into what he probably called his brain. He had decided on the evidence that I was Smooth Sam Fisher, and no denials on my part were going to shake his belief. He looked on them merely as so many unsportsmanlike quibbles, prompted by greed.

"Tell it to Sweeney!" was the form in which he crystallized his skepticism.

Then, with a sudden return to ferocity, "All right, you Sam, you wait! We'll fix you, and fix you good! See? Dat goes. You t'ink youse kin put it across us, huh? All right, you'll get yours. You wait!"

And with these words he slid off into the night. From somewhere in the murky middle distance came a scornful "Hawg!" and he was gone.

## Chapter 5
# FRONTAL ATTACK

That Buck Macginnis was not the man to let the grass grow under his feet in a situation like the present one I would have gathered from White's remarks, if I had not already done so from personal observation. The world is divided into dreamers and men of action. From what little I had seen of him, I placed Mr. Macginnis in the latter class.

I looked for frontal attack from Buck, not subtlety; but, when the attack came, it was so excessively frontal that my chief emotion was a sort of paralyzed amazement. It seemed incredible that such peculiarly Wild Western events could happen in peaceful England—even in so isolated a spot as Sanstead House.

It had been one of those interminable days which occur only at schools. A school, more than any other institution, is dependent on the weather. Every small boy rises from his bed of a morning charged with a definite quantity of mischief; and this, if he is to sleep the sound sleep of health, he has to work off somehow before bedtime. That is why the summer term is the one a master longs for, when the intervals between classes can be spent in the open. There is no pleasanter sight for an assistant master at a private school than that of a number of boys expending their venom harmlessly in the sunshine.

On this particular day snow had begun to fall early in the morning; and while his pupils would have been only too delighted to go out and roll in it by the hour, they were prevented from doing so by Mr. Abney's strict orders. No schoolmaster enjoys seeing his pupils running risks and catching cold, and just then Mr. Abney was especially definite on the subject. The disturbance which had followed Mr. Macginnis's nocturnal visit to the school had had the effect of giving violent colds to three of the boys. And, in addition to that, Mr. Abney himself was in his bed, looking on the world with watering eyes. His views, therefore, on playing in the snow as an occupation for boys were naturally prejudiced.

The result was that Glossop and I had to try to keep order among a mob of small boys, none of whom had had any chance of working off his superfluous energy.

Little by little, however, we had won through the day, and the boys had subsided into comparative quiet over their evening preparation, when from outside the front door there sounded the purring of the engine of a large automobile. The bell rang.

I heard White's footsteps crossing the hall, then the click of the latch, and then—a sound that I could not define. The closed door of the classroom deadened it, but for all that it was audible. It resembled the thud of a falling body, but I knew it could not be that, for, in peaceful England, butlers opening front doors do not fall with thuds.

My class, always ready to stop work for a friendly chat, found material in the sound for conversation.

"Sir, what was that, sir?"

"Did you hear that, sir?"

"What do you think's happened, sir?"

"Be quiet," I shouted. "Will you be——"

There was a quick footstep outside; the door flew open; and on the threshold stood a short, sturdy man in a motoring coat and cap. The upper part of his face was covered by a strip of white linen, with holes for the eyes, and there was a Browning pistol in his hand.

It is my belief that, if assistant masters were allowed to wear white masks and carry automatic pistols, keeping order in a school would become child's play. A silence such as I had never been able to produce fell instantaneously upon the classroom.

As for me, I was dazed. Motor bandits may terrorize France, and desperadoes hold up trains in America, but this was peaceful England. The fact that Buck Macginnis was at large in the neighborhood did not make the thing any the less incredible.

And yet it was the simple, even the obvious, thing for Buck to do. Given an automobile, success was certain. Sanstead House stood absolutely alone. There was not even a cottage within half a mile. A train broken down in the middle of the Bad Lands was not more cut off.

Consider, too, the peculiar helplessness of a school in such a case. A school lives on the confidence of parents, a nebulous foundation which the slightest breath can destroy. I do not suppose Mr. Macginnis had thought the thing out in all its bearings, but he could not have made a sounder move if he had been a Napoleon. Where the owner of an ordinary country house, raided by masked men, can raise the countryside in pursuit, a schoolmaster must do precisely the opposite. From his point of view, the fewer people that know of the affair the better. Parents are jumpy people. Golden-haired Willie may be receiving the finest education conceivable; yet, if men with Browning pistols are familiar objects at his shrine of learning, they will remove him.

I do not, as I say, suppose that Buck, whose *forte* was action rather than brain work, had thought all this out. He had trusted to luck, and luck had stood by him. There would be no raising of the countryside in his case. On the contrary, I could see Mr. Abney becoming one of the busiest persons on record in his endeavor to hush the thing up and prevent it getting into the papers.

The man with the pistol spoke. He sighted me—I was standing with my back to the mantelpiece, parallel with the door—made a sharp turn, and raised his weapon.

"Put 'em up, sport," he said.

It was not the voice of Buck Macginnis. I put my hands up.

He half turned his head to the class.

"Which of youse kids is Ogden Ford?"

The class was beyond speech. The silence continued.

"Ogden Ford is not here," I said.

Our visitor had not that simple faith which is so much better than Norman blood. He did not believe me. Without moving his head, he gave a long whistle. Steps sounded outside. Another short, sturdy form entered the room.

"He ain't in de odder room," observed the new comer. "I been rubberin'!"

This was friend Buck beyond question. I could have recognised his voice anywhere.

"Well, dis guy," said the man with the pistol, indicating me, "says he ain't here. What's de answer?"

"Why, it's Sam!" said Buck. "Howdy, Sam? Pleased to see us, huh? We're in on de ground floor, too, dis time, all right, all right."

His words had a marked effect on his colleague.

"Is dat Sam! Let me blow de head off'n him!" he said with simple fervor; and, advancing a step nearer, he waved his disengaged fist truculently. In my *rôle* of Sam I had plainly made myself very unpopular. I have never heard so much emotion packed into a few words.

Buck, to my relief, opposed the motion. I thought this decent of Buck.

"Cheese it," he said, curtly.

The other cheesed it. The operation took the form of lowering the fist. The pistol he kept in position.

Mr. Macginnis resumed the conduct of affairs.

"Now den, Sam," he said, "come across! Where's de kid?"

"My name is not Sam," I said. "May I put my hands down?"

"Yes, if you want the top of your head blown off."

Such was not my desire. I kept them up.

"Now den, you Sam," said Mr. Macginnis again, "we ain't got time to burn. Out wit it. Where's dat kid?"

Some reply was obviously required. It was useless to keep protesting that I was not Sam.

"At this time in the evening he is generally working with Mr. Glossop."

"Who's Glossop? Dat guy in de room over dere?"

"Exactly."

"Well, he ain't dere. I bin rubberin'. Aw, quit yer foolin', Sam, where is he?"

"I couldn't tell you just where he is at the present moment," I said precisely.

"Let me swat him one!" begged the man with the pistol. A most unlovable person. I could never have made a friend of him.

"Cheese it, you!" said Mr. Macginnis.

The other cheesed it once more, regretfully.

"You got him hidden away somewheres, Sam," said Mr. Macginnis. "You can't fool me. I'm goin' t'roo dis joint wit a fine-tooth comb, till I find him."

"By all means," I said. "Don't let me stop you."

"You! You're comin' with me."

"If you wish it, I shall be delighted."

"Say, why *mayn't* I hand him one?" demanded the pistol-bearer, "What's your kick against it?"

I thought the question in poor taste. Buck ignored it.

"Gimme dat canister," he said, taking the Browning pistol from him. "Now den, Sam, are youse goin' to be good, and come across, or ain't you, which?"

"I'd be delighted to do anything you wished, Mr. Macginnis," I said, "but——"

"Aw, hire a hall!" said Buck, disgustedly. "Step lively, den, and we'll go t'roo de joint."

Shooting pains in my shoulders caused me to interrupt him.

"One moment," I said. "I'm going to put my hands down. I'm getting cramp."

"I'll blow a hole in you if you do!"

"Just as you please. But I'm not armed."

"Lefty," he said to the other man, "feel around to see if he's carryin' anyt'ing."

Lefty advanced, and began to tap me scientifically in the neighborhood of my pockets. He grunted morosely the while. I suppose at this close range the temptation to "hand me one" was almost more than he could bear.

"He ain't got no gun," he announced, gloomily.

"Den youse can put 'em down," said Mr. Macginnis.

"Thanks," I said.

"Lefty, youse stay here and look after dese kids. Get a move on, Sam."

We left the room, a little procession of two, myself leading, Buck in my immediate rear administering occasional cautionary prods with the faithful "canister."

The first thing that met my eyes as we entered the hall was the body of a man lying by the front door. The light of the lamp fell on his face, and I saw that it was White. His hands and feet were tied. As I looked at him, he moved, as if straining against his bonds; and I was conscious of a feeling of relief. That sound that had reached me in the classroom, that thud of a falling body, had become, in the light of what had happened later, very sinister. It was good to know that he was still alive.

There was a masked man leaning against the wall by Glossop's classroom. He was short and sturdy. The Buck Macginnis gang seemed to have been turned out on a pattern. Externally, they might all have been twins. This man, to give him a semblance of individuality, had a ragged red moustache. He was smoking a cigar with the air of the warrior taking his rest.

"Hello!" he said, as we appeared. He jerked a thumb towards the classroom. "I've locked dem in. What's doin', Buck?" he asked, indicating me with a languid nod.

"We're going t'roo de joint," explained Mr. Macginnis. "De kid ain't in dere. Hump yourself, Sam!"

His colleague's languor disappeared with magic swiftness.

"Sam! Is dat Sam? Here, let me beat de block off'n him!"

Few points in this episode struck me as more remarkable than the similarity of taste which prevailed, as concerned myself, among the members of Mr. Macginnis's gang. Men, doubtless, of varying opinions on other subjects, on this one point they were unanimous. They all wanted to assault me.

Buck, however, had other uses for me. For the present I was necessary as a guide, and my value as such would be impaired were the block to be beaten off me. Though feeling no more friendlier towards me than did his assistants, he declined to allow sentiment to interfere with business. He concentrated his attention on the upward journey with all the earnestness of the young gentleman who carried the banner with the strange device in the poem.

Briefly requesting his ally to cheese it—which he did—he

urged me on with the nozzle of the pistol. The red-moustached man sank back against the wall again with an air of
dejection, sucking his cigar now like one who has had disap-
pointments in life, while we passed on up the stairs and
began to draw the rooms on the first floor.

These consisted of Mr. Abney's study and two dormitories. The study was empty, and the only occupants of the dormitories were the three boys who had been stricken down
with colds on the occasion of Mr. Macginnis's last visit. They
squeaked with surprise at the sight of the assistant master in
such questionable company.

Buck eyed them disappointedly. I waited, with something
of the feelings of a drummer taking a buyer round the sam-
ple room.

"Get on," said Buck.

"Won't one of those do?"

"Hump yourself, Sam."

"Call me Sammy," I urged. "We're old friends now."

"Don't get fresh," he said, austerely. And we moved on.

The top floor was even more deserted than the first.
There was no one in the dormitories. The only other room
was Mr. Abney's; and, as we came opposite it, a sneeze from
within told of the sufferings of its occupant.

The sound stirred Buck to his depths.

"Who's in dere?" he demanded.

"Only Mr. Abney. Better not disturb him. He has a bad
cold."

He placed a wrong construction on my solicitude for my
employer. His manner became excited.

"Open dat door, you," he cried.

No one who is digging a Browning pistol into the small of
my back will ever find me disobliging. I opened the door—
knocking first, as a mild concession to the conventions—and
the procession passed in.

My stricken employer was lying on his back, staring at the

ceiling, and our entrance did not at first cause him to change this position.

"Yes?" he said thickly, and disappeared beneath a huge pocket-handkerchief. Muffled sounds, as of distant explosions of dynamite, together with earthquake shudderings of the bedclothes, told of another sneezing fit.

"I'm sorry to disturb you," I began, when Buck, ever the man of action with a scorn for palaver, strode past me, and, having prodded with the pistol that part of the bedclothes beneath which a rough calculation suggested that Mr. Abney's lower ribs were concealed, uttered the one word, "Sa-a-ay!"

Mr. Abney sat up like a jack-in-the-box. One might almost say that he shot up. And then he saw Buck.

I cannot even faintly imagine what were Mr. Abney's emotions at that moment. He was a man who, from boyhood up, had led a quiet and regular life. Things like Buck had appeared to him hitherto, if they had appeared at all, only in dreams after injudicious suppers. Even in the ordinary costume of the Bowery gentleman, without such adventitious extras as masks and pistols, Buck was no beauty. With that hideous strip of dingy white linen on his face, he was a walking nightmare.

Mr. Abney's eyebrows had risen and his jaw had fallen to their uttermost limits. His hair, disturbed by contact with the pillow, gave the impression of standing on end. He stared at Buck, fascinated.

"Say, you, quit rubberin'. Youse ain't in a dime museum. Where's dat Ford kid, huh?"

I have set down all Mr. Macginnis's remarks as if they had been uttered in a bell-like voice with a clear and crisp ennunciation; but, in doing so, I have flattered him. In reality his mode of speech suggested that he had something large and unwieldy permanently stuck in his mouth; and it was not easy for a stranger to follow him. Mr. Abney signally failed to do so. He continued to gape helplessly, till the tension was broken by a sneeze.

One cannot interrogate a sneezing man with any satisfaction to oneself. Buck stood by the bedside in moody silence, waiting for the paroxysm to spend itself.

I, meanwhile, had remained where I stood, close to the door. And, as I waited for Mr. Abney to finish sneezing, for the first time since Buck's colleague Lefty had entered the classroom the idea of action occurred to me. Until this moment, I suppose, the strangeness and unexpectedness of these happenings had numbed my brain. To precede Buck meekly upstairs and to wait with equal meekness while he interviewed Mr. Abney had seemed the only course open to me. To one whose life has lain apart from such things, the hypnotic influence of a Browning pistol is irresistible.

But now, freed temporarily from this influence, I began to think; and, my mind making up for its previous inaction by working with unwonted swiftness, I formed a plan of action at once.

It was simple, but I had an idea that it would be effective. My strength lay in my acquaintance with the geography of Sanstead House and Buck's ignorance of it. Let me but get an adequate start, and he might find pursuit vain. It was this start which I saw my way to achieving.

To Buck it had not yet occurred that it was a tactical error to leave me between the door and himself. I suppose he relied too implicitly on the mesmeric pistol. He was not even looking at me.

The next moment my fingers were on the switch of the electric light, and the room was in darkness.

There was a chair by the door. I seized it, and swung it into the space between us. Then, springing back, I banged the door, and ran.

I did not run without a goal in view. My objective was the study. This, as I have explained, was on the first floor. Its window looked out on to a strip of lawn at the side of the house, ending in a shrubbery. The drop would not be pleasant, but I seemed to remember a waterspout that ran up the wall close to the window; and, in any case, I was not in a position to be deterred by the prospect of a bruise or two. I had not failed to realize that my position was one of extreme peril. When Buck, concluding the tour of the house, found that Ogden Ford was not there, as I had reason to know that he would—there was no room for doubt that he would withdraw the protection which he had extended to me up to the present in my capacity of guide. On me the disappointed fury of the raiders would fall. No prudent consideration for their own safety would restrain them. If ever the future was revealed to man, I saw mine. My only chance was to get out into the grounds, where the darkness would make pursuit an impossibility.

It was an affair which must be settled one way or the other in a few seconds; and I calculated that it would take Buck just those few seconds to win his way past the chair and find the door handle.

I was right. Just as I reached the study the door of the bedroom flew open, and the house rang with shouts and the noise of feet on the uncarpeted landing. From the hall below came answering shouts, but with an interrogatory note in them. The assistants were willing, but puzzled. They did not like to leave their posts without specific instructions, and Buck, shouting as he clattered over the bare boards, was unintelligible.

I was in the study, the door locked behind me, before they could arrive at an understanding. I sprang to the window.

The handle rattled. Voices shouted.

A panel splintered beneath a kick, and the door shook on its hinges.

And then, for the first time, I think, in my life, panic gripped me—the sheer blind fear which destroys the reason.

It swept over me in a wave, that numbing terror which comes to one in dreams. Indeed, the thing had become dreamlike. I seemed to be standing outside myself, looking on at myself, watching myself heave and strain with bruised fingers at a window that would not open.

## *Chapter 6*
# THE DISAPPEARANCE OF OGDEN

The armchair critic, reviewing a situation calmly and at his ease, is apt to make too small allowance for the effect of hurry and excitement on the human mind. I had lost my head, and had ceased for the moment to be a reasoning creature. In the end, indeed, it was no presence of mind but pure good luck which saved me. Just as the door, which had held out gallantly, gave way beneath the attack from outside, my fingers, slipping, struck against the catch of the window, and I understood why I had failed to raise it.

I snapped the catch back, and flung up the sash. An icy wind swept into the room, bearing particles of snow. I scrambled on to the window sill, and a crash from behind me told of the falling of the door.

The packed snow on the sill was drenching my knees as I worked my way out and prepared to drop. There was a deafening explosion inside the room, and simultaneously something seared my shoulders like a hot iron. I cried out with the pain of it, and, losing my balance, fell from the sill.

There was, fortunately for me, a laurel bush immediately below the window. I fell into it, all arms and legs. I was on my feet in an instant. The idea of flight, which had obsessed me a moment before to the exclusion of all other mundane affairs, had vanished absolutely. I was full of fight—I might say overflowing with it. I remember standing there with the snow trickling in chilly rivulets down my face and neck, and shaking my fist at the window. Two of my pursuers were leaning out of it, while a third dodged about behind them, like a small man on the outskirts of a crowd. So far from being thankful for my escape, I was conscious only of a feeling of regret that there was no immediate way of getting at them.

From the direction of the front door came the sound of one running. A sudden diminution of the noise of his feet told me that he had left the gravel and was on the turf. I drew back a pace or two and waited.

It was pitch dark, and I had no fear that I should be seen. I was standing well outside the light from the window.

The man stopped just in front of me. A short parley followed.

"Can'tja see him?"

The voice was not Buck's. It was Buck who answered. And when I realized that this man in front of me, within easy reach, on whose back I was shortly about to spring, and whose neck I proposed, under Providence, to twist into the shape of a corkscrew, was no mere underling but Mr. Macginnis himself, I was filled with a joy which I found it hard to contain in silence.

Looking back, I am a little sorry for Mr. Macginnis. He was not a good man. His mode of speech was not pleasant, and his manners were worse than his speech. But, though he undoubtedly deserved all that was coming to him, it was nevertheless bad luck for him to be standing there at just that moment.

He had got as far, in his reply, as "Naw, I can't——" when I sprang. I connected with Mr. Macginnis in the region of the waist, and we crashed to the ground together.

Our pleasures are never perfect. There is always something. In the program which I had hastily mapped out, the upsetting of Mr. Macginnis was but a small item, a mere preliminary.

There were a number of things which I had wished to do to him, once upset. But it was not to be. A compact form was already wriggling out on the window sill, as I had done, and I heard the grating of his shoes on the wall as he lowered himself for the drop.

There is a moment when the pleasantest functions must come to an end. I was loth to part from Mr. Macginnis just when I was beginning, as it were, to do myself justice; but it was unavoidable.

I disengaged myself—Mr. Macginnis strangely quiescent during the process—and was on my feet in the safety of the darkness just as the reinforcement touched earth. This time I did not wait. My hunger for fight had been appeased to some extent by my brush with Buck, and I was satisfied to have achieved safety with honor.

Making a wide detour, I crossed the drive and worked my way through the bushes to within a few yards of where the automobile stood, filling the night with the soft purring of its engines.

I had not been watching long before a little group advanced into the light of the automobile's lamps. There were four of them. Three were walking; the fourth was lying on their arms, of which they made something resembling a stretcher.

The driver of the car, who had been sitting woodenly in his seat, turned at the sound.

"Ja get him?" he inquired.

"Get nothing!" replied one of the three moodily. "De kid ain't dere, an' we was chasin' Sam to fix him, an' he laid for us, an' what he did to Buck was plenty."

They placed their burden in the tonneau, where he lay repeating himself, and two of them climbed in after him. The third seated himself beside the driver.

"Buck's leg's broke," he announced.

No young actor, receiving his first round of applause, could have felt a keener thrill of gratification than I did at these words. Life may have nobler triumphs than the breaking of a kidnapper's leg, but I did not think so then. It was with an effort that I stopped myself from cheering.

The car turned and began to move with increasing speed down the drive. Its drone grew fainter and ceased. I brushed the snow from my coat, and walked to the front door.

My first act, on entering the house, was to release White. He was still lying where I had seen him last. He appeared to have made no headway with the cords on his wrists and ankles. I came to his help with a rather blunt pocketknife, and he rose stiffly and began to chafe the injured arms in silence.

"They've gone," I said.

He nodded.

"I broke Buck's leg," I said, with modest pride.

He looked up incredulously. The gloom was swept from his face by a joyful smile. Buck's injury may have given its recipient pain, but it was certainly the cause of pleasure to others.

I had been vaguely conscious during this conversation of an intermittent noise like distant thunder. I now perceived that it came from Glossop's classroom, and was caused by the beating of hands on the door panels. I remembered that the red-moustached man had locked Glossop and his young charges in. I unlocked the door and the classroom, its occupants, headed by my colleague, disgorged in a turbulent stream. At the same moment my own classroom began to empty itself. The hall was packed with boys, and the din became deafening. Everyone had something to say, and they all said it at once.

Glossop's eyes gleamed agitatedly. Macbeth's deportment,

when confronted with Banquo's ghost, was stolid by comparison. There was no doubt that Buck's visit had upset the smooth peace of our happy little community to quite a considerable extent.

Small boys are always prone to make a noise, even without provocation. When they get a genuine excuse like the incursion of men in white masks, who prod assistant masters in the small of the back with Browning pistols, they tend to eclipse themselves. I doubt whether we should ever have quieted them, had it not been that the hour of Buck's visit had chanced to fall within a short time of that set apart for the boys' tea, and that the kitchen had lain outside the sphere of our visitors' operations. As in many English country houses, the kitchen at Sanstead House was at the end of a long corridor, shut off by doors through which even pistol shots penetrated but faintly. The cook had, moreover, the misfortune to be somewhat deaf, with the result that, throughout all the storm and stress in our part of the house, she, like the lady in Goethe's poem, had gone on cutting bread and butter; till now, when it seemed that nothing could quell the uproar, there rose above it the ringing of the bell.

If there is anything exciting enough to keep the Englishman or the English boy from his tea, it has yet to be discovered. The shouting ceased on the instant. The general feeling seemed to be that inquiries could be postponed till a more suitable occasion, but not tea. There was a general movement in the direction of the dining room.

I left Glossop to preside at the meal, and went upstairs to see Mr. Abney. It seemed to me that something in the nature of an official report ought to be made to him. It was his school that Mr. Macginnis and his friends had been kicking to pieces.

My tap upon his door produced an agitated "Who's that?" I reassured him, and there came from within the sound of moving furniture. His one brief interview with Buck had evidently caused my employer to ensure against a second by barricading himself in with everything he could lay his hands on.

"Cub id," said a voice at last. Mr. Abney was sitting up in bed, the blankets wrapped tightly about him. His appearance was still disordered. The furniture of the room was in great confusion, and a poker on the floor by the dressing table showed that he had been prepared to sell his life dearly.

"Bister Burds," he said, "what is the explanation of this extraordinary affair?"

"It was a gang of American kidnappers. They were after Ogden Ford. White tells me they have been after him for some time."

"White?" said Mr. Abney, puzzled.

It struck me that the time had come to reveal White's secret. Certainly the motive for concealing it—the fear of making Mr. Abney nervous—was removed. An inrush of Red Indians with tomahawks could hardly have added greatly to Mr. Abney's nervousness just at present.

"White is a detective," I said.

It took some time to make the matter thoroughly clear to Mr. Abney, but I had just done so when Glossop whirled into the room.

"Mr. Abney, Ogden Ford is nowhere to be found!"

Mr. Abney greeted the information with a prodigious sneeze.

"What do you bead?" he demanded, when the paroxysm was over. He turned to me. "Bister Burds, I understood you to—ah—say that the scou'drels took their departure without him?"

"They certainly did. I watched them go."

"I have searched the house thoroughly," said Glossop, "and there are no signs of him. And not only that—the boy Beckford cannot be found."

Mr. Abney clasped his head in his hands. Poor man, he was in no condition to bear up with easy fortitude against this succession of shocks. He was like one who, having survived an earthquake, is hit by an automobile. He had partly adjusted his mind to the quiet contemplation of Mr. Macginnis and friends, when he was called upon to face this fresh disaster. And he had a cold in the head, which unmans the stoutest. Napoleon would have won Waterloo if Wellington had had a cold in his head.

"The boy Beckford caddot be fou'd!" he echoed, feebly.

"They must have run away together," said Glossop.

Mr. Abney sat up, galvanized.

"Such a thi'g has dever happ'n'd id the school before!" he cried. "I caddot seriously credit the fact that Augustus Beckford, one of the bost charbi'g boys it has ever beed my good fortude to have id by charge, has deliberately rud away."

"He must have been persuaded by that boy Ford," said Glossop.

"Subthi'g bust be done at once," Mr. Abney exclaimed. "It is ibperative that we take ibbediate steps. They bust have gone to London." An idea struck him. "Bister Burds, tell White I wish to speak to him. Bister Glossop, I think you had better go back to the boys now. Please find White at once, Bister Burds."

I found White in the hall, and explained matters to him.

"Mr. Abney wants to see you," I said. "Ogden Ford has run away to London, and I think he wants you to go after him. I have told him who you are and why you are here. I hope you don't mind?"

"Not at all. I should have told him myself in any case, now that the necessity has arisen."

We went upstairs. Mr. Abney was sitting up in bed, waiting for us.

"Cub id, White," he said. "Bister Burds has just bade an—ah—extraordinary cobbudication to me. It seebs you are a—id fact—a detective."

"Yes, sir," said White.

"Sent here by Bister Ford?"

"Yes, sir."

"Exactly. Ah—precisely." He sneezed. "I do not cobbedt on the good taste or wisdob of Bister Ford's actiod id keeping the matter a secret and not i'forbing me. All that is beside the point. Ogden Ford and Augustus Beckford have rud away to Londod. I wish you, White, to follow them. I should be glad if you would accompady White, Bister Burds!"

"I don't think it necessary to trouble Mr. Burns," said White. "I am sure I can manage by myself."

"Two heads are better than wud."

"Too many cooks spoil the broth, sir."

"Dodseds," said Mr. Abney irritably, ending this interchange of proverbial wisdom with a sneeze. "Bister Burds will accompady you, as I say."

"Very well, sir."

And we left the room, to look out a train.

## Chapter 7
## SMOOTH SAM FISHER

As my first essay in detective work, I could have wished that the tracking down of Ogden Ford and his friend Augustus had been more of a feat, but I am bound to admit that it was a singularly soft job. Dr. Watson could have done it on his head. Even what little credit there was attached to the performance was not mine. It was White who made the suggestion that led to our success—namely, that we should find out the address of young Beckford's parents, and make inquiries there. We could not apply to Mr. Elmer Ford, he, White informed me, having returned to America.

I did not know the Beckfords' address, and it was too late to telegraph for it that night. I did so the next morning, and received the answer towards the middle of the afternoon. Augustus's mother lived in Eaton Square.

When we arrived there, shortly after four, the mystery of Augustus's departure from the spot which it had been Mr. Abney's constant endeavor to make him regard as a happy home was explained. Sounds of revelry from within greeted us on the doorstep. There was a children's party going on.

Mrs. Beckford received me warmly. I had explained, when giving my name to the butler, that I was from the school. White preferred to wait in the square during the interview.

"It was so kind of Mr. Abney to let Augustus come up for his sister's birthday and bring his friend with him," she said. "I did not like to ask him, but Augustus seems to have managed it all on his own account."

I respected Augustus's secret. It did not seem to me that there was anything to be gained by exposing him in the home circle. So long as I took him back, I had done my part.

"I happened to be coming to London today," I said, "so Mr. Abney asked me to bring Augustus and Ogden Ford back with me. I thought of catching the seven o'clock train. May I see Augustus for a moment?"

Mrs. Beckford led me to the drawing room. Some sort of dance was going on. There was Augustus, his face shining with honest joy, leading the revels, while against the far wall, wearing the *blasé* air of one for whom custom has staled the more obvious pleasures of life, leaned Ogden Ford.

The effect of my appearance on them was illustrative of their respective characters. Augustus turned bright purple, and fixed me with a horrified stare. Ogden winked.

The dance came to an end. Augustus stood goggling at me

and shuffling his feet. Ogden strolled up and accosted me like an old friend.

"Hello!" he said. "I was wondering if you or the hot-air merchant would blow in. Come to fetch us back?"

He looked kindly over his shoulder at Augustus.

"Better let him enjoy himself while he's here. There's no hurry, I guess, now you've found us; and he likes this sort of thing. As a matter of fact, we were coming back tonight in any case. I shan't be sorry. I wanted to see what this sort of thing was like over here in England, but I'm sorry I came now—I'm bored pallid. Couldn't we slip away somewhere? Got a cigarette?"

The airy way in which this demon boy handled what should have been—to him—an embarrassing situation irritated me. For all the effect my presence had on him, I might have been the potted palm against which he was leaning.

"I have not got a cigarette," I said.

He regarded me tolerantly.

"Got a grouch this evening, haven't you? You seem all worked up about something." His face lighted up. He produced from his pocket a crumpled, battered-looking cigarette. "Thought I hadn't one left," he said, happily. "I'd forgotten this. Well, see you later."

He disappeared, leaving me to find my way out and report to White.

White was walking up and down the pavement.

"It's all right," I said. "They're in there."

"Both of them?"

"Yes."

White expelled what seemed to be a breath of relief. I began to notice something strange in his manner—a suppressed excitement foreign to his usual stolid calm.

"Mr. Burns," he said, "let's get where we can talk. I've got something I want to say to you. I've got a proposition to make."

I looked at him in surprise. Could this be White, of the

rich voice and the measured speech? It was a stranger speaking—a brisk, purposeful stranger, with a marked American intonation.

"See here," he said, "we must get together over this business."

Perhaps it was the recollection of the same words in the mouth of Buck Macginnis that startled me. His eyes were gleaming with excitement, and he gripped my arm.

"Say, it's the chance of a lifetime," he went on. "Here's the kid up in London, and nobody knows where except you and me. If ever there was a case of fifty-fifty, this is it. I can't get away with him without your help, and it's the same with you. The only thing is to sit in at the game together and share out. Does it go? Think quick!" he said. "I guess this comes as a kind of surprise to you, but hustle your brain and get a hold on it. Maybe you never thought of anything like this before, but surely to goodness you can see now what a gilt-edged chance it is."

He met my bewildered gaze, and calmed down. He chuckled.

"I ought to have started by explaining," he said. "I guess this seems funny talk to you from a detective. I'm not a detective, sonny. You caught me with a gun in the school grounds, so I had to put up some tale. I'm no sleuth, though—take it from me. Do you remember my telling you of a fellow named Smooth Sam Fisher? I'm Sam."

## *Chapter 8*
# I DECLINE A BUSINESS OFFER

Smooth Sam Fisher! I gaped at him. He nodded.

"It's always been a habit of mine in these little matters," he went on, "to let other folks do the rough work, and chip in myself when they've cleared the way. It saves trouble and expense. I don't travel with a gang, like that bone-head Buck. What's the use of a gang? They only get tumbling over each other and spoiling everything. Look at Buck! Where is he? Down and out. While I——"

He smiled complacently. His manner annoyed me. I had adjusted my mind to the fact of his identity now, and I objected to his bland assumption that I was his accomplice.

"While you—what?" I said.

He looked at me in mild surprise.

"Why, I come in with you, sonny, and take my share like a gentleman."

"Do you!"

"Well, don't I?"

He looked at me in the half reproachful, half affectionate manner of the kind old uncle who reasons with a headstrong nephew.

"Young man," he said, "you surely aren't thinking you can put one over on me in this business? Tell me, you don't take me for that sort of ivory-skulled boob! Do you imagine for one instant, sonny, that I'm not next to every move in this game? Let's hear what's troubling you. You seem to have gotten some foolish ideas in your head. Let's talk it over quietly."

"If you have no objection—no," I said. "I don't want to talk to you, Mr. Fisher."

He looked at me shrewdly. Apparently I had not offended him, only made him cautious.

"The present arrangement of equal division," he said, "holds good, of course, only in the event of your doing the square thing by me. Let me put it plainly. We are either partners or competitors. I have given you the idea of taking this chance of kidnapping the Ford kid, and you may think you can do it without any help. Don't try it! Young man, I am nearly twice your age, and I have, at a modest estimate, about ten times as much worldly wisdom. And I say to you, don't miss this chance. You will be sorry if you do, believe me! Later on, when I am a rich man and my automobile splashes you with mud in Piccadilly, you will taste the full bitterness of remorse."

I looked at him as he stood, plump and rosy and complacent, puffing at his cigarette, and my heart warmed to the old ruffian. It was impossible to be angry with him. I might hate him as a represenatative—and a leading represen- tative—of one of the most contemptible trades on earth, but there was a sunny charm about the man himself which made it hard to feel hostile to him as an individual.

I burst out laughing.

"You're a wonder!" I said.

He beamed.

"Then you think, on consideration——?" he said. "Ex- cellent! We are partners! We will work this together. All I ask is that you rely on my wider experience of this sort of game to get the kid safely away and open negotiations with papa."

"I suppose your experience has been wide?" I said.

"Quite tolerably. Quite tolerably."

"Doesn't it ever worry you, the anxiety and misery you cause?"

"Purely temporary, both. And then look at it in another way. In a sense you might call me a human benefactor. I teach parents to appreciate their children. You know what parents are. Father loses a block of money in the City. When he reaches home, what does he do? He eases his mind by snapping at little Willie. Mother's new dress doesn't fit. What happens? Mother takes it out of William. And then one af- ternoon he disappears. The agony! The remorse! 'How could I ever have told our lost angel to stop his darned noise!' moans father. 'I struck him!' sobs mother. 'With this jewelled hand I spanked our vanished darling!' 'We were not worthy to have him!' they wail together. 'But oh, if we could but get him back!' Well, they do, they get him back as soon as ever they care to come across in unmarked hundred-dollar bills. And after that they think twice before working off their grouches on the poor kid. So I bring universal happiness into the home. I don't say father doesn't get a twinge every now and then when he catches sight of the hole in his bank balance, but, hang it, what's money for if it's not to spend?"

He snorted with altruistic fervor.

"What makes you so set on kidnapping Ogden Ford?" I asked. "I know he is valuable, but you must have made your pile by this time. I gather that you have been practicing your particular brand of philanthropy for a good many years. Why don't you retire?"

He sighed.

"It is the dream of my life to retire, young man. You may not believe me, but my instincts are thoroughly domestic. When I have the leisure to weave daydreams, they center around a cozy little home with a nice porch and stationary washtubs."

He regarded me closely, as if to decide whether I was worthy of these confidences. There was something wistful in his brown eyes. I suppose the inspection must have been favorable, as he was in a mood when a man must unbosom himself to someone, for he proceeded to open his heart to me. A man in his particular line of business, I imagine, finds few confidants, and the strain probably becomes intolerable at times.

"Have you ever experienced the love of a good woman, sonny? It's a wonderful thing." He brooded sentimentally for a moment, then continued, and—to my mind—somewhat spoiled the impressiveness of his opening words. "The love of a good woman," he said, "is about the darnedest wonderful layout that ever came down the pike. I know. I've had some."

A spark from his cigarette fell on his hand. He swore a startled oath.

"We came from the same old town," he resumed, having recovered from this interlude. "Used to be kids at the same school. Walk to school together. Me carrying her luncheon basket, and helping her over the fences. Ah! Just the same when we grew up. Still pals. And that was twenty years ago. The arrangement was that I should go out and make the money to buy the home, and then come back and marry her."

"Then why in the world haven't you done it?" I said, severely.

He shook his head.

"If you know anything about crooks, young man," he said, "you'll know that outside of their own line they are the easiest marks that ever happened. They fall for anything. At least, it's always been that way with me. No sooner did I get together a sort of pile and start out for the old town, when some smooth stranger would come along and steer me up against some skin-game, and back I'd have to go to work. That happened a few times, and when I did manage at last to get home with the dough, I found she had married another guy. It's hard on women, you see," he explained, chivalrously. "They get lonesome, and Roving Rupert doesn't show up, so they have to marry Stay-at-home Henry just to keep from getting the horrors."

"So she's Mrs. Stay-at-home Henry now?" I said, sympathetically.

"She was till a year ago. She's a widow now. I saw her just before I left to come here. She's as fond of me as ever. It's all settled, if only I can get the money. And she don't want much either. Just enough to keep the home together."

"I wish you happiness," I said. "What does she say to your way of making money?"

"She don't know. And she ain't going to know. I don't see why a man has got to tell his wife every little thing in his past. She thinks I'm a commercial traveler, traveling in England for a dry goods firm. She's very particular—always was. That's why I'm going to quit after I've won out over this business. And now that you are standing in——"

I shook my head.

"You won't?"

"I'm sorry to spoil a romance, but I can't. You must look around for some other home into which to bring happiness. The Fords' is barred."

"You are very obstinate, young man," he said sadly, but without any apparent ill-feeling "I can't persuade you?"

"No."

"Ah, well! So we are to be rivals, not allies. You will regret this, sonny. I may say you will regret it very bitterly. When you see me in my automo——"

"You mentioned your automobile before."

"Ah! So I did."

He drew at his cigarette thoughtfully.

"I don't understand you, young man. I don't know how much salary you get at the school, but I guess it's not particularly much. And there's no knowing what old man Ford wouldn't cough up, if you'd only stand in with me and leave me to work the negotiations. Yet you won't come in with me on this thing. Why?—that's what beats me. Why?"

"Call it conscience. If you know what that means."

"And you are really going to take him back to the school?"

"I am."

"Well, well," he sighed. "I hoped I had seen the last of the place. The English countryside may be delightful in the summer, but for winter give me London. However"—he sighed again resignedly—"shall we travel down together? What train did you think of taking?"

"Do you mean to say," I demanded, "that you have the cheek, the nerve, to come back to the school after what you have told me about yourself?"

"Did you think of exposing me to Mr. Abney? Forget it, young man. He would not believe you."

"It won't be hard to prove. All he will have to do will be to ask Mr. Ford if he did send a detective to Sanstead."

"Mr. Ford is in America."

"There is the cable."

"Don't try it. You would only waste your money. Mr. Ford's answer would be that he did send a detective. He was a man of the name of Dennis. A very intelligent man. It cost me a great deal of money—most of it, I admit, in promises—to induce him to throw up the job and stand in with me. How's Mr. Ford to know that I am not the man he sent? No, I think you will see, sonny, that you will not gain much by informing Mr. Abney. So tomorrow, after our little jaunt to London, we shall all resume the quiet rural life once more."

He beamed expansively upon me.

"However, even the quiet, rural life has its interests. I guess we shan't be dull."

I believed him.

## Chapter 9
# COFFEE, AND AN ANNOUNCEMENT

Considering the various handicaps under which he labored—notably a cold in the head and a fear of Ogden—Mr. Abney's handling of the situation, when the runaways returned to the school, bordered on the masterly. Having conscientious objections to corporal punishment, he fell back on oratory, and he did this to such effect that, when he had finished, Augustus Beckford wept openly, and was so subdued that he hardly spoke for days.

One result of the adventure was that Ogden's bed was

moved to a sort of cubbyhole adjoining my room. In the
house as originally planned, this had evidently been a dressing room. Under Mr. Abney's rule it had come to be used as
a general repository for lumber. My boxes were there, and a
portmanteau of Glossop's. It was an excellent place in which
to bestow a boy in quest of whom kidnappers might break in
by night. The window was too small to allow a man to pass
through, and the only means of entrance was by way of my
room. By night, at any rate, Ogden's safety seemed to be assured.

The curiosity of the small boy, fortunately, is not lasting.
His active mind lives mainly in the present. It was not many
days, therefore, before the excitement caused by Buck's raid
and Ogden's disappearance began to subside. Within a week
both episodes had been shelved as subjects of conversation,
and the school had settled down to its normal humdrum life.

In the days which followed, the behavior of Smooth Sam
Fisher puzzled me. I do not know just what I expected him
to do, but I certainly did not expect him to do nothing. Yet
time went on, and still he made no move. It was only by
reminding myself constantly that he was a man who believed
in waiting his opportunity that I kept myself from relaxing
my vigilance.

He was a fine actor. He knew that I was watching him, and
he knew that I was aware of this; yet never once, by so much
as a look, did he abandon the *rôle* he had set himself to play.
He was the very model of a butler. When he spoke to me,
the grave respect which he put into his voice at times almost
set me off my guard. I think that if I had had the information that he was a kidnapper from any other lips then his
own, I should have been unable to believe it. But our deal-
ings with one another in London had left me vigilant, and
his pose did not disarm me. His inaction sprang from pa-
tience: it was not due to any weakening of purpose or despair of success. Sooner or later, I knew, he would act swiftly
and suddenly, with a plan perfected in every detail.

I was right. But when he made his attack, it was the very simplicity of his methods that tricked me; and, but for a lucky chance, which no strategist could have foreseen and guarded against, I should have been defeated.

I have said that it was the custom of the staff of masters at Sanstead House School—in other words, of every male adult in the house except Mr. Fisher himself—to assemble in Mr. Abney's study after dinner of an evening to drink coffee. It was a ceremony—like most of the ceremonies at an establishment such as a school, where things are run on a schedule— which knew of no variation. Sometimes Mr. Abney would leave us immediately after the ceremony, but he never omitted to take his part in it first.

On this particular evening, for the first time since the beginning of the term, I was seized with a prejudice against coffee. I had been sleeping badly for several nights, and, searching for a remedy, I decided that abstention from coffee might help me.

I waited, for form's sake, till Glossop and Mr. Abney had filled their cups, then went to my room, where I lay down in the dark. From the room beyond came faintly the snores of the sleeping Ogden.

At this moment Smooth Sam Fisher had no place in my meditations. My mind was not occupied with him at all. When, therefore, the door, which had been ajar, began to open slowly, I did not become instantly on the alert, I attributed the movement to natural causes and wondered if it were worth while getting up to shut it.

The opening widened.

Perhaps it was some sound, barely audible, that aroused me from my torpor and set my blood tingling with anticipation. Perhaps it was the way the door was opening. An honest draught does not move a door furtively in jerks.

I sat up noiselessly, tense and alert. And then, very quietly, somebody entered the room.

There was only one man in Sanstead House who would

enter a room like that. I was amused. The impudence of the
thing tickled me. It seemed so foreign to Mr. Fisher's usual
cautious methods. This strolling in and helping oneself was
certainly kidnapping *de luxe*. In the small hours I could have
understood it; but at nine o'clock at night, with Glossop, Mr.
Abney, and myself awake and liable to be met at any moment on the stairs, it was absurd. I marveled at Smooth
Sam's effrontery.

I lay still. I imagined that, being in, he would switch on the
electric light. He did, and I greeted him pleasantly.

"And what can I do for *you*, Mr. Fisher?"

For a man who had learned to control himself in difficult
situations he took the shock badly. He uttered a startled
exclamation, and spun round, open-mouthed.

"I—I," he stammered, "I didn't know you were here."

"Quite a pleasant surprise. Do you want anything?"

I could not help admiring the quickness with which he recovered himself. Almost immediately he was the suave,
chatty Sam Fisher who had unbosomed his theories and
dreams to me in the train to London.

"I quit," he said, pleasantly. "The episode is closed. I
would not dream of competing with you, sonny, in a physical
struggle. And I take it that you would not keep on lying
quietly on that bed while I went into the other room and ab-
stracted our young friend? Or maybe you have changed
your mind again? Would a fifty-fifty offer tempt you?"

"Not an inch."

"No, no. So I suspected. I merely asked."

"And how about Mr. Abney, in any case? Suppose we met
him on the stairs?"

"We should not meet him on the stairs," said Sam, con-
fidently. "You did not take coffee tonight, I gather?"

"I didn't—no. Why?"

He jerked his head resignedly.

"Can you beat it! I ask you, young man, could I have

foreseen that, after drinking coffee every night regularly for two months, you would pass it by tonight of all nights?"

His words had brought light to me.

"Did you drug the coffee?"

"Did I! I fixed it so that one sip would have an insomnia patient in dreamland before he had time to say 'Good night.' That stuff Rip Van Winkle drank had nothing on my coffee. And all wasted! Well, well!"

He turned towards the door.

"Shall I leave the light on, or would you prefer it off?"

"On, please. I might fall asleep in the dark."

"Not you! And if you did, you would dream that I was there, and wake up. There are moments, young man, when you bring me pretty near to quitting and taking to honest work."

"Why don't you?"

"But not altogether. I have still a shot or two in my locker. We shall see what we shall see. I am not dead yet. Wait!"

"I will. And some day, when I am walking along Piccadilly, a passing automobile will splash me with mud. A heavily furred plutocrat will stare haughtily at me from the tonneau, and with a start of surprise I shall recognize——"

"Stranger things have happened. Be fresh while you can, sonny. You win so far, but this hoodoo of mine can't last for ever."

He passed from the room with a certain sad dignity. A moment later he reappeared.

"A thought strikes me," he said. "The fifty-fifty proposition does not impress you. Would it make things easier if I were to offer my cooperation for a mere quarter of the profits?"

"Not in the least."

"It's a handsome offer."

"It is. But I am not dealing on any terms."

He left the room only to return once more.

His head appeared, staring at me round the door in a disembodied way, like the Cheshire cat.

"You won't say later on I didn't give you your chance?"

He vanished again, permanently this time. I heard his steps passing down the stairs.

We had now arrived at the last week of term—at the last days of the last week. The vacation spirit was abroad in the school. Among the boys it took the form of increased disorderliness. Boys who had merely spilt ink now broke windows. Ogden Ford abandoned cigarettes in favor of an old clay pipe which he found in the stables.

Complete quiescence marked the deportment of Mr. Fisher during these days. He did not attempt to repeat his last effort. The coffee came to the study unmixed with alien drugs. Sam, like lightning, did not strike twice in the same place. He had the artist soul, and disliked patching up bungled work.

If he made another move, it would, I knew, be on entirely fresh lines.

Ignoring the fact that I had had all the luck, I was inclined to be self-satisfied when I thought of Sam. I had pitted my wits against his, and I had won. It was a praiseworthy performance for a man who had done hitherto nothing particular in his life.

If all the copy-book maxims which had been drilled into me in my childhood had not been sufficient, I ought to have been warned by Sam's advice not to take victory for granted till the fight was over. As Sam had said, his misfortunes could not last for ever. The luck would turn sooner or later.

One realizes these truths in theory, but the practical application of them seldom fails to come as a shock. I received mine on the last morning but one of the term.

Shortly after breakfast a message was brought to me that Mr. Abney would like to see me in his study. I went without any sense of disaster to come. Most of the business of the school was discussed in the study after breakfast, and I imagined that the matter had to do with some detail of the morrow's exodus.

I found Mr. Abney pacing the room, a look of annoyance on his face.

There was a touch of embarrassment in Mr. Abney's manner, for which I could not at first account. He coughed once or twice before proceeding to the business of the moment.

"Ah, Mr. Burns," he said at length, "might I ask if your plans for the holidays—the—ah—earlier part of the holidays—are settled?"

"No," I said; "I shall go to London for a day or two, I think."

He produced a letter from the heap of papers on the desk.

"Ah—excellent. That simplifies matters considerably. I have no right to ask what I am about to—ah—in fact, ask. I have no claim on your time in the holidays. But in the circumstances perhaps you may see your way to doing me a considerable service. I have received a letter from Mr. Elmer Ford, who landed in England yesterday morning, which puts me in a position of some difficulty. It is not my wish to disoblige the parents of the boys who are entrusted to my care, and I should like, if possible, to do what Mr. Ford asks. It appears that certain business matters call him to the North of England for a few days, thus rendering it impossible for him to receive little Ogden. I must say that a little longer notice would have been a—in fact, a convenience. But Mr. Ford, like so many of his countrymen, is what I believe is called a hustler. 'He does it now,' as the expression is. In short, he wishes to leave little Ogden at the school for the first few days of the holidays, and I should be extremely obliged, Mr. Burns, if you could find it possible to stay here and—ah—look after him."

Mr. Abney coughed again, and resumed.

"I would stay myself, but the fact is I am called to London on very urgent business."

He pressed the bell.

"In the event of your observing any suspicious characters in the neighborhood, you have the telephone, and can instantly communicate with the police. And you will have the assistance of——"

The door opened, and Smooth Sam Fisher entered.

"You rang, sir?"

"Ah! Come in, White, and close the door. I have something to say to you. I have just been informing Mr. Burns that Mr. Ford has written asking me to allow his son to stay on at the school for the first few days of the vacation. The whole arrangement is excessively unusual, and I may say—ah—disturbing. However, you have your duty to fulfill to your employer, White, and you will, of course, remain here with the boy."

"Yes, sir."

I found myself looking into a bright brown eye that gleamed with genial triumph. The other was closed. In the exuberance of the moment, Smooth Sam had had the bad taste to wink at me.

"You will have Mr. Burns to help you, White. He has kindly consented to postpone his departure during the short period in which I shall be compelled to be absent."

I had no recollection of having given any kind consent, but I was very willing to have it assumed. That wink had roused my fighting spirit.

I was glad to see that Mr. Fisher, though Mr. Abney did not observe it, was visibly taken aback by this piece of information. But he made one of his swift recoveries.

"It is very kind of Mr. Burns," he said, in his fruitiest voice, "but I hardly think it will be necessary to put him to the inconvenience of altering his plans. I am sure that Mr.

Ford would prefer the entire charge of the affair to be in my hands."

He had not chosen a happy moment for the introduction of the millionaire's name. Mr. Abney was a man of method, who hated any dislocation of the fixed routine of life; and Mr. Ford's letter had upset him. The Ford family, father and son, were just then extremely unpopular with him.

He crushed Sam.

"What Mr. Ford would or would not prefer is, in this particular matter, beside the point. The responsibility for the boy, while he remains on the school premises, is—ah—mine, and I shall take such precautions as seem fit and adequate to—h'm—myself, irrespective of those which, in your opinion, might suggest themselves to Mr. Ford. As I cannot be here myself, owing to—ah—urgent business in London, I shall certainly take advantage of Mr. Burns's kind offer to remain as my deputy."

"Very well, sir," said Sam meekly.

I spent the rest of the day in London, returning to Sanstead by the last train. Mr. Abney gave me leave reluctantly, for the request was certainly unusual. He asked me if it was absolutely essential that I should go to London. I said that it was. I thought so too. My object in making the journey was to buy a Browning pistol. I was taking no risks with Smooth Sam Fisher.

## Chapter 10
## EXIT AND REENTER SAM

A school during the holidays is a lonesome spot. There was a weirdly deserted air about the whole place when the last cab had rolled off on its way to the station. I roamed restlessly through the grounds with Ogden. A stillness brooded over everything, as if the place had been laid under a spell. Never before had I been so impressed with the isolation of Sanstead House. Anything might happen in this lonely spot, and the world would go on its way in ignorance.

It was not long before the inconveniences of my watchdog life began to be borne in upon me. Shortly after lunch I became aware that I needed tobacco, and that speedily, or the night would find me destitute. The nearest tobacconist's shop was two miles away, next door to the "Feathers." I had to have it, and yet I could not leave Ogden. I was obliged to take him with me, and a less congenial companion for a country walk I have never met. He loathed exercise, and said so in a number of ways until we reached the shop.

As we were coming out, a man emerged from the "Feathers." He growled unintelligibly, for I had nearly collided with him; then suddenly uttered an exclamation, and stared at Ogden.

There was no need for introductions. It was my much enduring acquaintance, Mr. Buck Macginnis.

The next moment he had moved off down the street. He walked quickly. His leg appeared to be restored to its old perfection.

I stood looking after him. The vultures were gathered together with a vengeance. Sam within, Buck without—it was quite like old times.

"We'll have a cab back to the house," I said to Ogden, who received the information with sombre pleasure.

It had occurred to me that Mr. Macginnis might have formed some idea of ambushing our little expedition on the way home.

My mind was active in the cab. It was not hard to account for Buck's reappearance. He would, of course, have made it his business to get early information of Mr. Ford's movements. It would be easy for him to discover that the millionaire had been called away to the North, and that Ogden was still an inmate of Sanstead House. And here he was, preparing for the grand attack.

I had been premature in removing Buck's name from the list of active combatants. Broken legs mend. I ought to have remembered that.

His presence on the scene made, I perceived, a vast difference to my plan of campaign. It was at this point that my purchase of the Browning pistol really appeared in the light of an acute strategic move. With Buck, that disciple of the frontal attack, in the field, there might be need for it.

Long before the cab drew up at the door of Sanstead House, I had made up my mind on the point of my next move. I proposed to eject Sam without delay. I had shrunk from this high-handed move till now, but the reappearance of Buck left me no choice.

I settled Ogden in the study, and went in search of him. He would, I imagined, be in the housekeeper's room—a cozy little apartment off the passage leading to the kitchen. I decided to draw that first, and was rewarded, on pushing open the half-closed door, by the sight of a pair of black-trousered legs stretched out before me from the depths of a wicker-work armchair. His portly middle section, rising beyond like a small hill, heaved rhythmically. His face was covered with a silk handkerchief, from beneath which came, in even succession, faint and comfortable snores. It was a peaceful picture—the good man taking his rest.

Pleasing as Sam was as a study in still life, pressure of business compelled me to stir him into activity. I prodded him gently in the center of the rising territory beyond the black trousers. He grunted discontentedly, and sat up. The handkerchief fell from his face. He blinked at me—at first with the dazed glassiness of the newly awakened, then with a "Soul's Awakening" expression, which spread over his face until it melted into a friendly smile.

"Hello, young man!"

"Good afternoon. You seem tired."

He yawned cavernously.

"Forty winks. It clears the brain."

"Had all you want?"

His face split in another mammoth yawn. He threw his heart into it, as if life held no other tasks for him. Only in alligators have I ever seen its equal.

"I guess I'm through," he said.

"Then out you get, Mr. Fisher."

"Eh?"

"Take your last glimpse of the old home, Sam, and out into the hard world."

He looked at me inquiringly. "You seem to be talking, young man. Words appear to be fluttering from you. But your meaning, if any, escapes me."

"My meaning is that I am about to turn you out. There is not room for both of us here. So, if you do not see your way to going quietly, I shall take you by the back of the neck and run you out. Do I make myself fairly clear now?"

He permitted himself a rich chuckle.

"You have gall, young man. Well, I hate to seem unfriendly. I like you, sonny. You amuse me—but there are moments when one wants to be alone. Trot along, kiddo, and quit disturbing uncle. Tie a string to yourself and disappear. Bye-bye."

The wicker-work creaked as he settled his stout body. He picked up a newspaper.

"Mr. Fisher," I said, "I have no wish to propel your gray hairs at a rapid run down the drive, so I will explain further. I mean to turn you out. How can you prevent it? Mr. Abney is away. You can't appeal to him. The police are at the end of the telephone, but you can't appeal to them. As you said yourself, you can't compete with me in a physical struggle. So what *can* you do except go? Do you get me now?"

He regarded the situation in thoughtful silence. He allowed no emotion to find expression in his face, but I knew that the signfiance of my remarks had sunk in. I could al-

most follow his mind, as he tested my position point by
point, and found it impregnable.

When he spoke it was to accept defeat jauntily.

"Very well, young man. Just as you say. You're really set
on my going? Say no more. I'll go. After all it's quiet at the
inn, and what more does a man want?"

The day dragged on. I spent the greater part of it walking
about the grounds. Towards night the weather broke suddenly after the fashion of spring in England. Showers of
rain drove me to the study.

It must have been nearly ten o'clock when the telephone
rang.

It was Sam.

"Hello, is that you, Mr. Burns?"

"It is. Do you want anything?"

"I want a talk with you. Business. Can I come up? I'm at
'The Feathers.'"

"If you wish it."

"I'll start right away."

It was some fifteen minutes later that I heard in the distance the engine of an automobile. The headlights gleamed
through the trees, and presently the car swept round the
bend of the drive and drew up at the front door. A portly
figure got down and rang the bell. I observed these things
from a window on the first floor overlooking the front steps,
and it was from this window that I spoke.

"Is that you, Mr. Fisher?"

He backed away from the door.

"Where are you?"

"Is that your car?"

"It belongs to a friend of mine."

"I didn't know you meant to bring a party."

"There's only three of us. Me, the chauffeur, and my
friend—Macginnis."

The possibility, indeed the probability, of Sam seeking out

Buck and forming an alliance had occurred to me, and I was prepared for it. I shifted my grip on the automatic pistol in my hand.

"Mr. Fisher."

"Hello?"

"Ask your friend Macginnis to be good enough to step into the light of that lamp, and drop his pistol."

## Chapter 11
## CUT OFF

There was a muttered conversation. I heard Buck's voice rumbling like a train going under a bridge. The request did not appear to find favor with him. Then came an interlude of soothing speech from Mr. Fisher. I could not distinguish the words, but I gathered that he was pointing out to him that, on this occasion only, the visit being for purposes of parley and not to attack, pistols might be looked on as non-essentials. Whatever his arguments they were successful, for, finally, humped as to the back and muttering, Buck appeared in the spotlight.

"Good evening, Mr. Macginnis," I said. "I'm glad to see your leg is all right again. I won't detain you a moment. Just feel in your pockets and shed a few of your guns, and then you can come in out of the rain. To prevent any misunderstanding, I may say I have a gun of my own. It is trained on you now."

"I ain't got no gun."

"Come along. This is no time for airy persiflage. Out with them."

A moment's hesitation, and a small black pistol fell to the ground.

"No more?"

"Think I'm a regiment?"

"I don't know what you are. Well, I'll take your word for it. You will come in one by one with your hands up."

I went down and opened the door, holding my pistol in readiness against the unexpected.

Sam came first. His raised hands gave him a vaguely pontifical air (Bishop blessing Pilgrims), and the kindly smile he wore heightened the illusion. Mr. Macginnis, who followed, suggested no such idea. He was muttering moodily to himself, and he eyed me askance.

I showed them into the classroom, and switched on the light. The air was full of many odors. Disuse seems to bring out the inky, chalky, appley, deal-boardy bouquet of a classroom as the night brings out the scent of flowers. During the term I had never known this classroom smell so exactly like a classroom. I made use of my free hand to secure and light a cigarette.

Sam rose to a point of order.

"Young man," he said, "I should like to remind you that we are here, as it were, under a flag of truce. To pull a gun on us and keep us holding our hands up this way is raw work. I feel sure I speak for my friend, Mr. Macginnis."

He cocked an eye at his friend Mr. Macginnis, who seconded the motion by expectorating into the fireplace.

"Mr. Macginnis agrees with me," said Sam, cheerfully. "Do we take them down? Have we your permission to assume position two of these Swedish exercises? All we came for was a little friendly chat among gentlemen, and we can talk just as well—speaking for myself, better—in a less strained attitude. A little rest, Mr. Burns? A little folding of the hands? Thank you."

He did not wait for permission; nor was it necessary. Sam and the melodrama atmosphere were as oil and water. It was impossible to blend them. I laid the pistol on the table and sat down. Buck, after one wistful glance at the weapon, did the same. Sam was already seated, and was looking so cozy and at home that I almost felt it remiss of me not to have provided sherry and cake for this pleasant gathering.

"Well," I said, "what can I do for you?"

"Let me explain," said Sam. "As you have no doubt gathered, Mr. Macginnis and I have gone into partnership."

"I gathered that. Well?"

"Judicious partnerships are the soul of business. Mr. Macginnis and I have been rivals in the past, but we both saw that the moment had come for an alliance. We form a strong team. My partner's speciality is action. I supply the strategy. Say, sonny, can't you see you're up against it? Why be foolish?"

"You think you're certain to win?"

"It's a cinch."

"Then why trouble to come here and see me?"

I appeared to have put into words the smouldering thought which was vexing Mr. Macginnis. He burst into speech.

"Sure! What's de use? Didn't I tell youse? What's de use of wastin' time? What are we spielin' away here for? Let's get busy."

Sam waved a hand towards him with the air of a lecturer making a point.

"You see! The man of action! He likes trouble. He asks for it. Now I prefer peace. Why have a fuss when you can get what you want quietly? That's my motto. That's why we've come. It's the old proposition. We're here to buy you out. Yes, I know you have turned the offer down before, but things have changed. Your stock has fallen. In fact, instead of letting you in on sharing terms, we only feel justified now in offering a commission. For the moment you may seem to hold a strong position. You are in the house, and you have got the boy. But there's nothing to it really. We could get him in five minutes if we cared to risk having a fuss. We should win dead easy all right if it came to trouble; but, on the other hand, you've a gun, and there's a chance some of us might get hurt; so what's the good when we can settle it quietly? How about it, sonny?"

Mr. Macginnis began to rumble, preparatory to making further remarks on the situation, but Sam waved him down and turned his brown eye inquiringly on me.

"Fifteen per cent is our offer," he said.

"And to think it was once fifty-fifty!"

"Strict business!"

"Business! It's sweating!"

"It's our limit. And it wasn't easy to make Buck here agree to that. He kicked like a mule."

Buck shuffled his feet, and eyed me disagreeably. I suppose it is hard to think kindly of a man who has broken your leg. It was plain that, with Mr. Macginnis, bygones were by no means bygones.

I rose.

"Well, I'm sorry you should have had the trouble of coming here for nothing. Let me see you out. Single file, please."

Sam looked aggrieved.

"You turn it down?"

"I do."

"One moment. Let's have this thing clear. Do you realize what you're up against? Don't think it's only Buck and me you've got to tackle. All the boys are here, waiting around the corner, the same gang that came the other time. Be sensible, sonny. You don't stand a dog's chance. I shouldn't like to see you get hurt. And you never know what may not happen. The boys are pretty sore at you because of what you did that night. I shouldn't act like a bonehead, sonny—honest."

There was a kindly ring in his voice which rather touched me. Between him and me there had sprung up an odd sort of friendship. He meant business, but he would, I knew, be genuinely sorry if I came to harm. And I could see that he was quite sincere in his belief that I was in a tight corner and that my chances against the combine were infinitesimal. I imagine that, with victory so apparently certain, he had had difficulty in persuading his allies to allow him to make his offer.

But he had overlooked one thing—the telephone. That he should have made this mistake surprised me. If it had been Buck, I could have understood it. Buck's was a mind which lent itself to such blunders. From Sam I had expected better things, especially as the telephone had been so much in evidence of late. He had used it himself only half an hour ago.

I clung to the thought of the telephone. It gave me the quiet satisfaction of the gambler who holds the unforeseen ace. The situation was in my hands. The police, I knew, had been profoundly stirred by Mr. Macginnis's previous raid. When I called them up, as I proposed to do directly the door had closed on the ambassadors, there would be no lack of response. It would not again be a case of Inspector Bones and Constable Johnson to the rescue. A great cloud of willing helpers would swoop to our help.

With these thoughts in my mind, I answered Sam pleasantly but firmly.

"I'm sorry I'm unpopular, but all the same——"

I indicated the door.

Emotion that could only be expressed in words and not through his usual medium welled up in Mr. Macginnis. He sprang forward with a snarl, falling back as my faithful automatic caught his eye.

"Say, you! Listen here! You'll——"

Sam, the peaceable, plucked at his elbow.

"Nothing doing. Step lively."

Buck wavered, then allowed himself to be drawn away. We passed out of the classroom in our order of entry.

I opened the front door, and they passed out. The automobile was still purring on the drive. Buck's pistol had disappeared. I suppose the chauffeur had picked it up, a surmise which proved to be correct a few moments later, when, just as the car was moving off, there was a sharp crack, and a bullet struck the wall to the right of the door. It was a random shot, and I did not return it. Its effect on me was to send me into the hall with a leap that was almost a back somersault. Somehow, though I was keyed up for violence and the shooting of pistols, I had not expected it at just that moment, and I was disagreeably surprised at the shock it had given me. I slammed the door and bolted it. I was intensely irritated to find that my fingers were trembling.

I went straight to the study, and unhooked the telephone.

There is apt to be a certain leisureliness about the methods of country telephone operators, and the fact that a voice did not immediately ask me what number I wanted did not at first disturb me. Suspicion of the truth came to me, I think, after my third shout into the receiver had remained unanswered. I had suffered from delay before, but never such delay as this.

I must have remained there fully two minutes, shouting at intervals, before I realized the truth. Then I dropped the receiver and leaned limply against the wall. For the moment I was as stunned as if I had received a blow. I could not even think. I took up the receiver again, and gave another call. There was no reply.

They had cut the wires.

# Chapter 12
# THE FIRST ROUND

I reviewed my position. Daylight would bring relief, for I did not suppose that even Buck Macginnis would care to conduct a siege which might be interrupted by the arrival of tradesmen in their carts and other visitors; but while the darkness lasted I was completely cut off from the world. With the destruction of the telephone wire my only link with civilization had been snapped. Even had the night been less stormy than it was, there was no chance of the noise of our warfare reaching the ears of anyone who might come to the rescue. It was as Sam had said; Buck's energy united to his strategy formed a strong combination.

Broadly speaking, there are only two courses open to a beleaguered garrison. It can stay where it is, or it can make a sortie. I considered the second of these courses.

It was possible that Sam and his allies had departed in the automobile to get reinforcements, leaving the coast temporarily clear; in which case, by escaping from the house at once, I might be able to get Ogden away unobserved through the grounds and reach the village in safety. To support this theory there was the fact that the car, on its late visit, had contained only the chauffeur and the two ambassadors, while Sam had spoken of the remainder of Buck's gang as being in readiness to attack in the event of my not coming to terms. That might mean that they were waiting at Buck's headquarters, wherever those might be—at one of the cottages down the road, I imagined—and, in the interval before the attack began, it might be possible for us to make our sortie with success.

I strained my eyes at the window, but it was impossible to see anything. The rain was still falling heavily. If the drive had been full of men, they would have been invisible to me.

I decided to make the sortie. Ogden was in bed. He woke when I shook him, and sat up, yawning the aggrieved yawns of one roused from his beauty sleep.

"What's all this?" he demanded.

"Listen," I said. "Buck Macginnis and Smooth Sam Fisher have come after you. They are outside now. Don't be frightened."

He snorted derisively.

"Who's frightened? I guess they won't hurt *me*. How do you know it's them?"

"They have just been here. The man who called himself White, the butler, was really Sam Fisher. He has been waiting his opportunity to get you all the term."

"White! Was he Sam Fisher?" He chuckled admiringly. "Say, he's a wonder!"

"They have gone to fetch the rest of the gang."

"Why don't you call the cops?"

"They have cut the wire."

His only emotions at the news seemed to be amusement and a renewed admiration for Smooth Sam. He smiled broadly, the little brute.

"He's a wonder!" he repeated. "I guess he's smooth all right. He's the limit! He'll get me all right this trip. I bet you a nickel he wins out."

I found his attitude trying. That he, the cause of all the trouble, should be so obviously regarding it as a sporting contest got up for his entertainment, was hard to bear. And the fact that, whatever might happen to myself, he was in no danger, comforted me not at all. If I could have felt that we were in any way companions in peril, I might have looked on the bulbous boy with quite a friendly eye. As it was, I nearly kicked him.

"Are you ready?" I said. "We have no time to waste."

"What's that?"

"We are going to steal out through the back way, and try to slip through to the village."

Ogden's comment on the scheme was brief and to the point. He did not embarrass me with fulsome praise of my strategic genius.

"Of all the fool games!" he said, simply. "In this rain? No, *sir!*"

This new complication was too much for me. In planning

out my maneuvers I had taken his cooperation for granted. I had looked on him as so much baggage—the impediment of the retreating army. And, behold, a mutineer!

I took him by the scruff of the neck and shook him. It was a relief to my feelings and a sound move. The argument was one which he understood.

"Oh, all right," he said. "Anything you like. Come on. But it sounds to me like darned foolishness."

If nothing else had happened to spoil the success of that sortie, Ogden's depressing attitude would have done so. Of all things, it seems to me, a forlorn hope should be undertaken with a certain enthusiasm and optimism if it is to have a chance of being successful. Ogden threw a gloom over the proceedings from the start. He was cross and sleepy, and he condemned the expedition unequivocally. As we moved towards the back door he kept up a running stream of abusive comment. I silenced him before cautiously unbolting the door, but he had said enough to damp my spirits. I do not know what effect it would have had on Napoleon's tactics if his army—say, before Austerlitz—had spoken of his maneuvers as "a fool game," and of himself as a "big chump," but I doubt if it would have stimulated him.

The back door of Sanstead House opened on to a narrow yard, paved with flagstones and shut in on all sides but one by walls. To the left was the outhouse where the coal was stored—a squat, barn-like building; to the right a wall that appeared to have been erected by the architect in an outburst of pure whimsicality. It just stood there. It served no purpose that I had ever been able to discover, except to act as a cats' club house.

Tonight, however, I was thankful for this wall. It formed an important piece of cover. By keeping in its shelter it was possible to work round the angle of the coal shed, enter the stable yard, and, by making a detour across the football field, avoid the drive altogether. And it was the drive, in my opinion, that might be looked on as the danger zone.

Ogden's complaints, which I had momentarily succeeded in checking, burst out afresh as the rain swept in at the opened door and lashed our faces. Certainly it was not an ideal night for a ramble. The wind was blowing through the opening at the end of the yard with a compressed violence due to the confined space. There was a suggestion in our position of the Cave of the Winds under Niagara Falls, the verisimilitude of which was increased by the stream of water that poured down from the gutter above our heads. Ogden found it unpleasant, and said so shrilly.

I pushed him out into the storm, still protesting, and we began to creep across the yard. Halfway to the first point of importance of our journey, the corner of the coal shed, I halted the expedition. There was a sudden lull in the wind, and I took advantage of it to listen.

From somewhere beyond the wall, apparently near the house, sounded the muffled note of the automobile. The siege party had returned.

There was no time to be lost. Apparently the possibility of a sortie had not yet occurred to Sam, or he would hardly have left the back door unguarded; but a general of his astuteness was certain to remedy the mistake soon, and our freedom of action might be a thing of moments. It behooved us to reach the stable yard as quickly as possible. Once there we should be practically through the enemy's lines.

Administering a kick to Ogden, who showed a disposition to linger and talk about the weather, I moved on, and we reached the corner of the coal shed in safety.

We had now arrived at the really perilous stage in our journey. Having built his wall to a point level with the end of the coal shed, the architect had apparently wearied of the thing and given it up, for it ceased abruptly, leaving us with a matter of half a dozen yards of open ground to cross, with nothing to screen us from the watchers on the drive. The flagstones, moreover, stopped at this point. On the open space was loose gravel. Even if the darkness allowed us to make the crossing unseen, there was the risk that we might be heard.

It was a moment for a flash of inspiration, and I was waiting for one, when that happened which took the problem out of my hands. From the interior of the shed on our left there came a sudden scrabbling of feet over loose coal, and through the square opening in the wall, designed for the peaceful purpose of taking in sacks, climbed two men. A pistol cracked. From the drive came an answering shout. We had been ambushed.

I had misjudeged Sam. He had not overlooked the possibility of a sortie.

It is the accidents of life that turn the scale in a crisis. The opening through which the men had leaped was scarcely a couple of yards behind the spot where we were standing. If they had leaped fairly and kept their feet they would have been on us before we could have moved. But Fortune ordered it that, zeal outrunning discretion, the first of the two should catch his foot in the woodwork and fall on all fours, while the second, unable to check his spring, alighted on top of him, and, judging from the stifled yell which followed, must have kicked him in the face.

In the moment of their downfall I was able to form a plan and execute it.

I clutched Ogden, and broke into a run; and we were across the open space and in the stable yard before the first of the men in the drive loomed up through the darkness. Half of the wooden double-gate of the yard was open, and the other half served us as a shield. They fired as they ran—at random, I think, for it was too dark for them to have seen us clearly—and two bullets slapped against the gate. A third struck the wall above our heads, and ricochetted off into the night. But before they could fire again we were in the stables, the door slammed behind us, and I had dumped Ogden on the floor, and was shooting the heavy bolts into their places. Footsteps clattered over the flag-stones, and stopped outside. Some weighty body plunged against the door. Then there was silence. The first round was over.

## *Chapter 13*
## ROUND TWO

The stables, as is the case in most English country houses, had been, in its palmy days, the glory of Sanstead House. In whatever other respect the British architect of that period may have fallen short, he never scamped his work on the stables. He built them strong and solid, with walls fitted to repel the assaults of the weather, and possibly those of men as well; for the Boones in their day had been mighty owners of race horses at a time when men with money at stake did not stick at trifles, and it was prudent to see to it that the spot where the favorite was housed had something of the na-ture of a fortress. The walls were thick, the door solid, the windows barred with iron. We could scarcely have found a better haven of refuge.

Under Mr. Abney's rule the stables had lost their original character. They had been divided into three compartments, each separated by a stout wall. One compartment became a gymnasium, another the carpenter's shop, the third, in which we were, remained a stable, though in these degen-erate days no horse ever set hoof inside it, its only use being to provide a place for the odd-job man to clean shoes. The mangers which had once held fodder were given over now to brushes and pots of polish. In term-time bicycles were stored in the loose box which had once echoed to the tram-pling of Derby favorites.

I groped about among the pots and brushes, and found a candle end, which I lit. I was running a risk, but it was necessary to inspect our ground. I had never troubled really to examine this stable before, and I wished to put myself in touch with its geography.

I blew out the candle, well content with what I had seen. The only two windows were small, high up, and excellently barred. Even if the enemy fired through them, there were half a dozen spots where we should be perfectly safe. Best of all, in the event of the door being carried by assault, we had a second line of defence in a loft. A ladder against the back wall led to it, by way of a trap door. Circumstances had certainly been kind to us in driving us to this apparently impregnable shelter.

On concluding my inspection, I became aware that Ogden was still occupied with his grievances. I think the shots must have stimulated his nerve centers, for he had abandoned the languid drawl with which, in happier moments, he was wont to comment on life's happenings, and was dealing with the situation with a staccato brightness.

"Of all the darned fool layouts I ever struck this is the limit. What do those idiots think they're doing, shooting us up that way? It went within an inch of my head. It might have killed me. Gee, and I'm all wet! I'm catching cold. It's all through your foolishness bringing us out here. Why couldn't we stay in the house?"

"We could not have kept them out of the house for five minutes," I explained. "We can hold this place."

"Who wants to hold it? *I* don't. What does it matter if they do get me? *I* don't care. I've a good mind to walk straight out through that door and let them rope me in. It would serve dad right. It would teach him not to send me away from home to any darned school again. What did he want to do it for? I was all right where I was. I——"

A loud hammering on the door cut off his eloquence. The intermission was over and the second round had begun.

It was pitch dark in the stable now that I had blown out the candle, and there is something about a combination of noise and darkness which tries the nerves. If mine had remained steady, I should have ignored the hammering. From the sound, it appeared to be made by some wooden instrument—a mallet from the carpenter's shop, I discovered later—and the door could be relied on to hold its own without any intervention. For a novice to violence, however, to maintain a state of calm inaction is the most difficult feat of all. I was irritated and worried by the noise, and I exaggerated its importance. It seemed to me that it must be stopped at once.

A moment before I had bruised my shins against an empty packing case, which had found its way with other lumber into the stable. I groped for this, swung it noiselessly into position beneath the window, and, standing on it, looked out. I found the catch of the window, and opened it. There was nothing be seen, but the sound of the hammering became most distinct; and, pushing an arm through the bars, I emptied my pistol at a venture.

As a practical move, the action had flaws. The shots cannot have gone anywhere near their vague target. But as a demonstration it was a wonderful success.

The yard became suddenly full of dancing bullets. They struck the flagstones, bounded off, chipped the bricks of the far wall, ricochetted to from those, buzzed in all directions, and generally behaved in a manner calculated to unman the stoutest-hearted.

The siege party did not stop to argue. They stampeded as one man. I could hear them clattering across the flagstones to every point of the compass. In a few seconds silence prevailed, broken only by the swish of the rain. Round two had been brief, hardly worthy to be called a round at all, and, like round one, it had ended wholly in our favor.

I jumped down from my packing case, swelling with pride. I had had no previous experience of this sort of thing, yet here I was handling the affair like a veteran. I considered that I had a right to feel triumphant. I lit the candle again, and beamed protectively upon Ogden.

He was sitting on the floor gaping feebly, and awed for the moment into silence.

"I didn't hit anybody," I announced, "but they ran like rabbits. They are all over Hampshire."

I was pleased with myself. I laughed indulgently. I could afford an attitude of tolerant amusement towards the enemy.

"They'll come back," said Ogden, morosely.

"Possibly. And in that case——" I felt in my left-hand coat pocket. "I had better be getting ready." I felt in my right-hand coat pocket.

A clammy coldness took possession of me.

"Ready," I repeated blankly. My voice trailed off into nothingness. For in neither pocket was there a single one of the shells with which I had fancied that I was abundantly provided.

In moments of excitement Man is apt to make mistakes. I had made mine when starting out on the sortie. I had left all my ammunition in the house.

# Chapter 14
# ROUND THREE, AND LAST

I should like to think that it was an unselfish desire to spare my young companion anxiety that made me keep my discovery to myself. But I am afraid that my reticence was due far more to the fact that I shrank from letting him discover my imbecile carelessness. Even in times of peril one retains one's human weaknesses, and I felt that I could not face his com-

ments. If he had permitted a certain note of querulousness
to creep into his conversation already, the imagination re-
coiled from the thought of the caustic depths he would
reach now, should I reveal the truth.

I tried to make things better with cheery optimism.

"*They* won't come back," I said stoutly; and tried to believe
it.

Ogden, as usual, struck the jarring note.

"Well, then, let's beat it," he said. "I don't want to spend
the night in this wretched icehouse. I tell you I'm catching
cold. My chest's weak. If you're so dead certain you've scared
them away let's quit."

I was not prepared to go so far as this.

"They may be somewhere near, hiding."

"Well, what if they are? I don't mind being kidnapped.
Let's go."

"It would be madness to go out now."

"Oh, pshaw," said Ogden, and from this point onwards
punctuated the proceedings with a hacking cough.

I had never really believed that my demonstration had
brought the siege to a definite end. I anticipated that there
would be some delay before the renewal of hostilities, but I
was too well acquainted with Buck Macginnis's tenacity to
imagine that he would abandon his task because a few random shots had spread momentary panic in his ranks. He
had all the night before him, and sooner or later he would
return.

I had judged him correctly. Many minutes dragged wea-
rily by without a sign from the enemy. Then, listening at the
window, I heard footsteps crossing the yard and voices talking in cautious undertones. The fight was on once more.

A bright light streamed through the window, flooding the
opening and spreading in a wide circle on the ceiling. It was
not difficult to understand what had happened. They had
gone to the automobile and come back with one of the head-

lamps, an astute move, in which I seemed to see the finger of Sam.

The danger spot thus rendered harmless, they renewed their attack on the door with a reckless vigor. The mallet had been superseded by some heavier instrument—of iron this time. I think it must have been the jack from the automobile. It was a more formidable weapon altogether than the mallet, and even our good oak door quivered under it.

A splintering of wood decided me that the time had come to retreat to our second line of entrenchments. How long the door would hold it was impossible to say, but I doubted if it were more than a matter of minutes.

Relighting my candle, which I had extinguished from motives of economy, I caught Ogden's eye, and jerked my head towards the ladder.

"Up you get," I whispered.

He eyed the trap door coldly, then turned to me with an air of resolution.

"If you think you're going to get me up there, you've another guess coming. I'm going to wait here till they get in, and let them take me. I'm about tired of this foolishness."

It was no time for verbal argument. I collected him, a kicking handful, bore him to the ladder, and pushed him through the opening. He uttered one of his devastating squeals. The sound seemed to encourage the workers outside, like a trumpet blast. The blows on the door redoubled.

I climbed the ladder, and shut the trap door behind me.

The air of the loft was close and musty, and smelt of mildewed hay. It was not the sort of spot which one would have selected of one's own free will to sit in for any length of time. There was a rustling noise, and a rat scurried across the rickety floor, drawing a startled yelp from Ogden. Whatever merits this final refuge might have as a stronghold, it was beyond question a noisome place.

The beating on the stable door was working up to a crescendo. Presently there came a crash that shook the floor on which we sat and sent our neighbors, the rats, scuttling to and fro in a perfect frenzy of perturbation. The light of the automobile lamp poured in through the numerous holes and chinks which the passage of time had made in the old boards. There was one large hole near the center which produced a sort of searchlight effect, and allowed us for the first time to see what manner of place it was in which we had entrenched ourselves. The loft was high and spacious. The roof must have been some seven feet above our heads. I could stand upright without difficulty.

In the proceedings beneath us there had come a lull. The mystery of our disappearance had not baffled the enemy for long, for almost immediately the rays of the lamp had shifted and began to play on the trap door. I heard some-body climb the ladder, and the trap door creaked gently as a hand tested it. I had taken up a position beside it, ready, if the bolt gave way, to do what I could with the butt of my pistol, my only weapon. But the bolt, though rusty, was strong, and the man dropped to the ground again. Since then, except for occasional snatches of whispered conversation, I had heard nothing.

Suddenly Sam's voice spoke.

"Mr. Burns."

I saw no advantage to remain silent.

"Well?"

"Haven't you had enough of this? You've given us a mighty good run for our money, but you can see for yourself that you're through now. I'd hate like anything for you to get hurt. Pass the kid down, and we'll call it off."

He paused.

"Well?" he said "Why don't you answer?"

"I did."

"Did you? I didn't hear you."

"I smiled."

"You mean to stick it out? Don't be foolish, sonny. The boys here are mad enough at you already. What's the use of getting yourself in the bad for nothing? We've got you in a pocket. I know all about that gun of yours, young fellow. I had a suspicion what had happened, and I've been into the house and found the shells you forgot to take with you. So, if you were thinking of making a bluff in that direction, forget it."

The exposure had the effect I had anticipated.

"Of all the chumps!" exclaimed Ogden, caustically. "You ought to be in a home. Well, I guess you'll agree to end this foolishness now? Let's go down and get it over and have some peace. I'm getting pneumonia."

"You're quite right, Mr. Fisher," I said. "But don't forget I still have the pistol, even if I haven't the shells. The first man who tries to come up here will have a headache tomorrow."

"I shouldn't bank on it, sonny. Come along, kiddo! You're done. Be good, and own it. We can't wait much longer."

"You'll have to try."

Buck's voice broke in on the discussion, quite unintelligible except that it was obviously wrathful.

"Oh, well!" I heard Sam say, resignedly, and then there was silence again below.

I resumed my watch over the trap door, encouraged. This parleying, I thought, was an admission of failure on the part of the besiegers. I did not credit Sam with a real concern for my welfare—thereby doing him an injustice. I can see now that he spoke perfectly sincerely. The position, though I was unaware of it, really was hopeless, for the reason that, like most positions, it had a flank as well as a front. In estimating the possibilities of attack I had figured assault as coming only from below. I had omitted from my calculations the fact that the loft had a roof.

It was a scraping on the tiles above my head that first brought the new danger point to my notice. There followed the sound of heavy hammering, and with it came a sickening realization of the truth of what Sam had said. We were beaten.

I was too paralyzed by the unexpectedness of the attack to form any plan; and, indeed, I do not think that there was anything that I could have done. I was unarmed and helpless. I stood there, waiting for the inevitable.

Affairs moved swiftly. Plaster rained down on the wooden floor. I was vaguely aware that the boy was speaking, but I did not listen to him.

A gap appeared in the roof, and widened. I could hear the heavy breathing of the man as he wrenched at the tiles.

And then the climax arrived, with anticlimax following so swiftly upon it that the two were almost simultaneous. I saw the worker on the roof cautiously poise himself in the opening, hunched up like some strange ape. The next moment he had sprung.

As his feet touched the floor there came a rending, splintering crash; the air was filled with a choking dust; and he was gone. The old worn-out boards had shaken under my tread. They had given way in complete ruin beneath this sharp onslaught. The rays of the lamp, which had filtered in little pencils of light through crevices, now shone in a great lake in the center of the floor.

In the stable below all was confusion. Everybody was speaking at once. The hero of the late disaster was groaning noisily—for which he certainly had good reason. I did not know the extent of his injuries, but a man does not do that sort of thing with impunity.

The next of the strange happenings of the night now occurred.

I had not been giving Ogden a great deal of my attention for some time, other and more urgent matters occupying me. His action at this juncture, consequently, came as a complete and crushing surprise.

I was edging my way cautiously towards the jagged hole in the center of the floor, in the hope of seeing something of what was going on below, when from close beside me his voice screamed: "It's me, Ogden Ford. I'm coming"; and, without further warning, he ran to the hole, swung himself over, and dropped.

Manna falling from the skies in the wilderness never received a more wholehearted welcome. Howls and cheers and ear-splitting whoops filled the air. The babel of talk broke out again. Some exuberant person found expression of his joy in emptying his pistol at the ceiling, to my acute discomfort, the spot he had selected as a target chancing to be within a foot of where I stood. Then they moved off in a body, still cheering.

## *Chapter 15*
# THE HAPPY ENDING

In my recollections of that strange night there are wide gaps. Trivial incidents come back to me with extraordinary vividness; while there are hours of which I can remember nothing. What I did or where I went I cannot recall. It seems to me, looking back, that I walked about the school grounds without a pause till morning. I lost, I know, all count of time. I became aware of the dawn as something that had happened suddenly, as if light had succeeded darkness in a flash. It had been night. I looked about me, and it was day—a steely, cheerless day, like a December evening. And I found that I was very cold and very tired.

I sat down on the stump of a tree. I must have fallen asleep, for, when I raised my eyes again, the day was brighter. Its cheerlessness had gone. The sky was blue and birds were singing.

It must have been an hour later before the first beginnings

of a plan of action came to me. It seemed to me that the only thing left to do was to go to London, find Mr. Abney, and report to him.

I turned to walk to the station. I could not guess even remotely what time it was. The sun was shining through the trees, but in the road outside the grounds there were no signs of workers beginning the day.

It was half-past five when I reached the station. A sleepy porter informed me that there would be a train to London at six.

I failed to find Mr. Abney. I inquired at his club, and was told that he had been there on the previous day, but not since then. I remained in London two days, calling at the club at intervals without success, and on the third returned to Sanstead. I could think of no other move.

It was about an hour after my return, and I was wandering about the grounds, trying to kill time, when there came the sound of automobile wheels on the gravel. A large red car was coming up the drive. It slowed down, and stopped beside me. There was only one passenger in the tonneau, a tall woman, smothered in furs. My main impression of her was of a pair of large, imperious eyes. That was all that there was of her, except furs.

I was given no leisure for wondering who she might be. Almost before the car had stopped she jumped out and clutched me by the arm, at the same time uttering this cryptic speech: "Whatever he offers I'll double!"

She fixed me, as she spoke, with a commanding eye. She was a woman, I gathered in that instant, born to command. There seemed, at any rate, no doubt in her mind that she could command me. If I had been a black beetle, she could not have looked at me with a more scornful superiority. Her eyes were very large and of a rich, fiery brown color.

"Bear that in mind," she went on. "I'll double it if it's a million dollars."

"I'm afraid I don't understand," I said finding speech.

She clicked her tongue impatiently.

"There's no need to be so cautious and mysterious. I'm Mrs. Elmer Ford. I came here directly I got your letter. I think you're the lowest sort of scoundrel that ever managed to keep out of jail, but that needn't make any difference just now. We're here to talk business, Mr. Fisher, so we may as well begin."

I was getting tired of being taken for Smooth Sam.

"My name is Burns," I said.

"*Alias* Sam Fisher?"

"Not at all. Plain Burns. I am—"

Mrs. Ford interrupted me. She gave me the impression of being a woman who wanted a good deal of the conversation and who did not care how she got it. In a conversational sense, she thugged me at this point. Or, rather, she swept over me like some tidal wave, blotting me out.

"Mr. Burns?" she said, fixing her brown eyes, less scornful now, but still imperious, on mine. "I must apologize. I have made a mistake. I took you for a low villain of the name of Sam Fisher. I was to have met him at this exact spot, just about this time, by appointment; so, seeing you here, I mistook you for him."

She stopped and raked me with her eyes, which said plainly, "If you are not Fisher, what earthly business have you here?"

"I am one of the assistant masters at the school," I said.

"Yes?"

"Mr. Abney left me to look after your son while he was away."

"Oh!"

She gave me a glance of unfathomable scorn.

"And you let this Fisher scoundrel steal him away from under your nose!" she said.

This was too much. I might be a worm, as her way of looking at me seemed to imply, but I felt the time had come to exercise a worm's prerogative of turning. This was one of the most unpleasant women I had ever met, and I saw no necessity for trying to spare her feelings.

"May I describe the way in which I allowed your son to be stolen away from under my nose?" I said. And in well-chosen words I sketched the outline of what had happened. I did not omit to lay stress on the fact that Ogden's departure with the enemy had been entirely voluntary.

She heard me out in silence.

"That was too bad of Oggie," she said tolerantly, when I had ceased dramatically at the climax of my tale.

As a comment it seemed to me inadequate.

"Oggie was always high-spirited," she went on. "No doubt you have noticed that?"

"A little."

"He could be led, but never driven. With the best intention, no doubt, you refused to allow him to leave the stable that night and return to the house, and he resented the check and took the matter into his own hands." She broke off, and looked at her watch. "Have you a watch? What time is it? Only that? I thought it must be later. I arrived too soon. I got a letter from this man Fisher, naming this spot and this hour for a meeting, when we could discuss terms. He said that he had written to Mr. Ford, appointing the same time." She frowned. "I have no doubt he will come," she said, coldly.

"Perhaps this is his car," I said.

A second automobile was whirring up the drive. There was a shout as it came within sight of us, and the chauffeur put on the brake. A man sprang from the tonneau. He jerked a word to the chauffeur and the car went on up the drive.

He was a massively built man of middle age, with powerful shoulders and a face—when he had removed his motorgoggles—very like any one of half a dozen of those Roman emperors whose features have come down to us on coins and statues—square-jawed, clean-shaven, and aggressive. Like his wife (who was now standing, drawn up to her full height, staring haughtily at him), he had the airs of one born to command. The clashing of those wills must have smacked of a collision between the immovable mass and the irresistible force.

He met Mrs. Ford's stare with one equally militant, then turned to me.

"I'll give you double what she has offered you," he said. He paused, and eyed me with loathing. "You scoundrel!" he added.

Custom ought to have rendered me immune to irritation, but it had not. I spoke my mind.

"One of these days, Mr. Ford," I said, "I am going to publish a directory of the names and addresses of the people who have mistaken me for Smooth Sam Fisher. I am *not* Sam Fisher. Can you grasp that? My name is Burns, and I am a master at this school. And I may say that, judging from what I know of the little beast, anyone who kidnapped your son as long as two days ago will be so anxious to get rid of him that he will probably want to pay you for taking him back."

My words almost had the effect of bringing this estranged couple together again. They made common cause against me.

"How dare you talk like that!" said Mrs. Ford. "Oggie is a sweet boy in every respect."

"You're perfectly right, Ruth," said Mr. Ford. "He may want intelligent handling, but he's a mighty fine boy."

"I shall make inquiries, Elmer, and if this man has been ill-treating Oggie, I shall complain to Mr. Abney."

"Quite right, Ruth."

"I always opposed the idea of sending him away from home. If you had listened to me this would not have happened."

"I'm not sure you aren't right. Where the dickens is this man Fisher?" he broke off abruptly.

"On the spot," said an affable voice. The bushes behind me parted, and Smooth Sam stepped out on to the gravel.

I had recognized him by his voice. I certainly should not have done so by his appearance. He had taken the precaution of "making up" for this important meeting. A white wig of indescribable respectability peeped out beneath his black hat, his eyes twinkled from under two penthouses of white eyebrows. A white moustache covered his mouth. He was venerable to a degree.

He nodded to me, and bared his white head gallantly to Mrs. Ford.

"No worse for our little outing, Mr. Burns, I am glad to see. Mrs. Ford, I must apologize for my apparent unpunctuality, but I was not really behind time. I have been waiting in the bushes. I thought it just possible that you might have brought unwelcome members of the police force with you, and I have been scouting, as it were, before making my advance. I see, however, that all is well, and we can come at once to business. May I say, before we begin, that I overheard your recent conversation, and that I entirely disagree with Mr. Burns. Master Ford is a charming boy. Already I feel like an elder brother to him. I am loth to part with him."

"How much?" snapped Mr. Ford. "You've got me. How much do you want?"

"I'll give you double what he offers!" cried Mrs. Ford.

Sam held up his hand, his old pontifical manner intensified by the white wig.

"May I speak? Thank you. This is a little embarrassing. When I asked you both to meet me here, it was not for the purpose of holding an auction. I had a straightforward business proposition to make to you. It will necessitate a certain amount of plain and somewhat personal speaking. May I proceed? Thank you. I will be as brief as possible."

His eloquence appeared to have had a soothing effect on the two Fords. They remained silent.

"You must understand," said Sam, "that I am speaking as an expert. I have been in the kidnapping business many years, and I know what I am talking about. And I tell you that the moment you two separated, you said good-bye to all peace and quiet. Bless you"—Sam's manner became fatherly—"I've seen it a hundred times. Couple separate, and, if there's a child, what happens? They start in playing battle-dore-and-shuttlecock with him. Wife sneaks him from husband. Husband sneaks him back from wife. After a while, along comes a gentleman in my line of business, a professional at the game, and he puts one across on both the amateurs. He takes advantage of the confusion, slips in, and gets away with the kid. That's what has happened here, and I'm going to show you the way to stop it another time. Now I'll make you a proposition. What you want to do"—I have never heard anything so soothing, so suggestive of the old family friend healing an unfortunate breach, as Sam's voice at this juncture—"what you want to do is to get together again right quick. Never mind the past. Let bygones be bygones."

A snort from Mr. Ford checked him for a moment, but he resumed.

"I guess there were faults on both sides. Get together and talk it over. And when you've agreed to call the fight off and start fair again, that's where I come in. Mr. Burns here will tell you, if you ask him, that I'm anxious to quit this business and marry and settle down. Well, see here. What you want to do is to give me a salary—we can talk figures later on—to stay by you and watch over the kid. Don't snort—I'm talking plain sense. You'd a sight better have me with you than against you. Set a thief to catch a thief. What I don't know about the fine points of the game isn't worth knowing. I'll guarantee, if you put me in charge, to see that nobody comes within a hundred miles of the kid unless he has an order-to-view. You'll find I earn every penny of that salary. Mr. Burns and I will now take a turn up the drive while you think it over."

He linked his arm in mine, and drew me away. As we turned the corner of the drive I caught a glimpse over my shoulder of Ogden's parents. They were standing where we had left them, as if Sam's eloquence had rooted them to the spot.

"Well, well, well, young man," said Sam eyeing me affectionately, "it's pleasant to meet you again, under happier conditions than last time. You certainly have all the luck, sonny, or you would have been badly hurt that night. I was getting scared how the thing would end. Buck's a plain roughneck, and his gang are as bad as he is, and they had got mighty sore at you—mighty sore. If they had grabbed you there's no knowing what might not have happened. However, all's well that ends well, and this little game has surely had the happy ending. I shall get that job, sonny. Old man Ford isn't a fool, and it won't take him long, when he gets to thinking it over, to see that I'm right. He'll hire me."

"Aren't you rather reckoning without your partner?" I said. "Where does Buck Macginnis come in on the deal?"

"He doesn't, sonny, he doesn't. It was a shame to do it—it was like taking candy from a kid—but business is business. I was reluctantly compelled to double cross poor old Buck. I sneaked the kid away from him next day. It's not worth talking about; it was too easy. Buck's all right in a rough-and-tumble, but when it comes to brains he gets left, and so he'll go on through life, poor fellow. I hate to think of it."

He sighed. Buck's misfortunes seemed to move him deeply.

"I shouldn't be surprised if he gave up the profession after this. He has had enough to discourage him. I told you about what happened to him that night, didn't I? No? I thought I had. Why, Buck was the guy who did the high dive through the roof; and, when we picked him up, we found he'd broken his leg again! Isn't that enough to jar a man? I guess he'll retire from the business after that. He isn't intended for it."

We were approaching the two automobiles now; and, looking back, I saw Mr. and Mrs. Ford walking up the drive. Sam followed my gaze, and I heard him chuckle.

"It's all right," he said. "They've fixed it up. Something in the way they're walking tells me they've fixed it up."

"Jarvis," she said to the chauffeur, "take the car home. I shan't need it anymore. I am going with Mr. Ford."

She stretched out a hand towards the millionaire. He caught it in his, and they stood there, smiling foolishly at each other, while Sam, almost purring, brooded over them like a stout fairy queen. The two chauffeurs looked on woodenly.

Mr. Ford released his wife's hand, and turned to Sam.

"Fisher!"

"Sir?"

"I've been considering your proposition. There's a string tied to it."

"Oh, no, sir. I assure you!"

"There is. What guarantee have I that you won't double cross me?"

Sam smiled, relieved.

"You forget that I told you that I was about to be married, sir. My wife won't let me!"

Mr. Ford waved his hand towards the automobile.

"Jump in," he said, briefly. "And tell him where to drive to. You're engaged!"

# The Wire-Pullers
# (A Cricket Story)

It is a splendid thing to be seventeen and have one's hair up and feel that one cannot be kissed indiscriminately anymore by sticky boys and horrid old gentlemen who "knew you when you were *that* high, my dear," or who nursed you on their knees when you were a baby. When I came down to dinner for the first time in a long frock and with my hair in a bun there was a terrific sensation. Father said, "My dear Joan!" and gasped. The butler looked volumes of respectful admiration. The tweeny, whom I met on the stairs, giggled like an idiot. Bob, my brother, who is a beast, rolled on the floor and pretended to faint. Altogether it was an event. Mr. Garnet, who writes novels and things and happened to be stopping with us for the cricket, asked me to tell him exactly how it felt to have one's hair up for the first time. He said it would be of the utmost value to him to know, as it would afford him a lurid insight into the feminine mind.

I said: "I feel as if I were listening to beautiful music played very softly on a summer night, and eating heaps of strawberries with plenty of cream."

He said, "Ah!"

But somehow I was not satisfied. The dream of my life

was to spend the winter in town, as soon as I had put my hair up, and go to dances and theatres and things, and regularly come out *properly*, instead of lingering on in this out-of-the-way place (which is ducky in the spring and summer, but awful in the winter), with nobody to be looked at by except relations and father and the curate and village doctors, and that sort of people.

We knew lots of nice people in town who would have given me a splendid time; but father was always too lazy to go. He hates London really. What he likes is to be out of doors all day and every day all the year round with his gun or rod. And he loves cricket, too. So do I. That is to say, I like watching it. But you can't watch cricket in the winter.

It really wasn't fair of father to keep me stowed away in a place like Much Middlefold now that I was grown up. I spoke to him about it after dinner.

I said, "Father, dear, you *are* going to take me to town this winter, aren't you?"

He shied. It is the only word to express it.

"Er—well, my dear—well, we'll see, we'll see."

Poor old father, he does hate London so. It always brings on his rheumatism or something, and he spends most of his time there, I believe, when he is really obliged to go up on business, mooning about Kensington Gardens, trying to make believe it's really the country. But there are times when one feels that other people's objections must give way. When a girl is pretty (I believe I am) and has nice frocks (I know I have), it is perfectly criminal not to let her go and show them in town. And I love dancing. I want to go to dances every night. And in Much Middlefold we have only the hunt ball, and perhaps, if we're lucky, two or three other dances. And you generally have to drive ten miles to them.

So I was firm.

I said, "Father, dear, why can't we settle it now, and then you could write and get a house in good time?"

He jibbed this time. He sat in his chair and said nothing.

"Will you, father?"

"But the expense——"

"You can let the Manor."

"And the land; I ought to be looking after it."

"Oh, but the tenant man who takes the house will do that. Won't you write tonight, father, dear? I'll write if you'll tell me what to say. Then you needn't bother to move."

Here an idea seemed to strike him. I noticed with regret that his face brightened.

"I'll tell you what, my dear," he said; "we will make a bargain."

"Yes," I said. I knew something horrid was coming.

"If I make fifty in the match on Monday, we will celebrate the event by spending the winter in town, much as I shall dislike it. Those wet pavements always bring on my rheumatism; don't know why. Wet grass never does."

"And if you don't make fifty, father?"

"Why then," he replied, cheerfully, "we'll stay at home and enjoy ourselves."

The match that was to be played on Monday was against Sir Edward Cave's team. Sir Edward was a nasty little man who had made a great deal of money somehow or other and been knighted for it. He always got together a house party to play cricket, and it was our great match. Sir Edward was not popular in the county, but he took a great deal of trouble with the cricket, and everybody was glad to play in his park or watch their friends playing.

Father always played for Much Middlefold in this match. He had been very good in his time, and I heard once that, if only the captain had not had so many personal friends for whom he wanted places in the team, father would have played for Oxford against Cambridge in his last year. But, of course, he was getting a little old now for cricket, and the Castle Cave match was the only one in which he played.

He had made twenty-five last year against Sir Edward Cave's team, and everybody had said how well he played, so I thought he might easily do better this year and make double that score.

"And if you make fifty you really will take me to town? You'll promise faithfully?"

*"Foi de gentilhomme!* The word of a Romney, my dear Joan; and, mind, if I do not make fifty the subject must be dropped for the present year of grace. Next year the discussion may be reopened; but for this winter there must be no further attempt at coaxing. You know that I am as clay in your hands, young woman, and you must not take an unfair advantage of my weakness."

I promised.

"And you really will try, father, to make fifty?"

"I can promise you that, my dear. It would take more than the thought of the horrors of London to make me get out on purpose."

So the thing was settled.

I went to see Bob about it before going to bed. Bob is a Freshman at Magdalen, so, naturally, he is much more conceited than any three men have any right to be. I suppress him when I can, but lately, in the excitement of putting my hair up, I had forgotten to give him much attention, and he had had a bad relapse.

I found him in the billiard room with Mr. Garnet. He was sprawling over the table, trying to reach his ball without the rest, and looking ridiculous. I waited till he had made his stroke and missed the red ball, which he ought to have pocketed easily.

Then I said, "Bob!"

He said, "Well, what?"

I think he must have been losing, for he was in a very bad temper.

"I want to speak to you."

"Go ahead, then."

I looked at Mr. Garnet. He understood at once.

"I'm just going to run upstairs for a second, Romney," he said. "I want my pipe. Cigarettes are bad for the soul. I sha'n't be long."

He disappeared.

"Well?" said Bob.

"Father says that if he makes fifty on Monday against the Cave he'll take me to London for the winter."

Bob lit another cigarette and threw the match out of the window.

"You needn't hurry to pack," he said.

"Don't you think father will make fifty?"

"He hasn't an earthly."

"He made twenty-five last year."

"Yes; but this year the Cave men have got a new pro. I don't suppose you have ever heard of him, but his name's Simpson—Billy Simpson. He played for Sussex all last season, and was eleventh in the first-class bowling averages. The governor may have been the dickens of a bat in his day, but I'll bet he doesn't stand up to Billy for many overs. As for getting fifty——"

Words failed him. I felt like a cat. I could have scratched somebody—anybody; I did not care whom. No wonder father had made the bargain so cheerfully. He knew he could only lose by a miracle.

"Oh, Bob!" I said. My despair must have been tremendous, for it touched even Bob. He said, "Buck up!"

I said, "I won't buck up. I think everybody's horrid."

"Look here," said Bob, anxiously—I could see by his face that he thought I was going to cry—"look here, chuck playing the giddy goat and going into hysterics and that sort of thing, and I'll give you a straight tip."

"Well?"

"This man Simpson—I have it on the highest authority—is in love with your maid—what's her name?"

"Saunders?"

"Saunders. At present it's a close thing between him and a chap in the village. So far it's anybody's race. Billy leads at present, because it's summer and he's a celebrity in the cricket season. But he must pull it off before the winter or he'll be pipped, because the other Johnny plays footer and is a little tin god in these parts directly footer begins. Why don't you get Saunders to square Billy and make him bowl the governor some tosh which he can whack about?"

"Bob," I cried, "you're an angel, and I'm going to kiss you!"

"Here, I say!" protested Bob. "Break away!"

While I was kissing him Mr. Garnet came back.

"They never do that to me," I heard him murmur, plaintively.

I spoke to Saunders while she was brushing my hair.

I said, "Saunders!"

"Yes, miss."

"Er—oh, nothing."

"Yes, miss."

There was a pause.

"Saunders!" I said.

"Yes, miss."

"Do you know Simpson, the cricket professional at Castle Cave?"

"Yes, miss."

Her face, reflected in the glass in front of me, grew pinker. It is always rather pink.

"He is very fond of you, isn't he?"

"He says so, miss."

She simpered—visibly.

"He would do anything for you, wouldn't he?"

"He says so, miss." Then, in a burst of confidence, "He said so in poetry once, miss."

We paused again.

"Saunders!" I said.

"Yes, miss."

"Would you like that almost new hat of mine? The blue chiffon one with the pink roses?"

She beamed. I believe her mouth watered.

"Oh, yes, miss."

Then I set out my dark scheme. I explained to her, having first shown her how necessary it was to keep it all quite secret, that a visit to town that winter depended principally on whether Mr. Simpson bowled well or badly in the match on Monday. She held Simpson in the hollow of her hand. Therefore she must prevail upon him to bowl father a sufficient quantity of easy balls to allow him to make fifty runs. In return for these services he would win Saunders's favor, and Saunders would win the hat she coveted and also a trip to London.

Saunders quite saw it.

She said, "Yes, miss."

"You must *make* him bowl badly," I said.

"I'll do what I can, miss. And I do really think that Mr. Simpson will act as I tells him to."

Once more she simpered.

Father came back in very good spirits from practicing at the village nets next day.

"I was almost in my old form, my dear," he said. "I was watching them all the way. Why, I am beginning to think I shall make that fifty after all."

I said, "So am I, father, dear."

Saunders had stirring news on the following night. It seemed that Mr. Simpson was in an awkward position.

"Sir Edward, miss," said Saunders," who always behaves

very handsome, Mr. Simpson says, has offered to give him a
ten-pound note if he bowls so well that nobody of the Middlefold side makes fifty against Castle Cave."

Here was a blow. I could not imagine any love being proof
against such a bribe. London seemed to get farther away as I
listened.

"And what does Simpson——"

"Well, Mr. Simpson and me, miss, we talked it over, and I
said, 'Oh, if you prefer Sir Edward's old money to a loving
heart,' I said, 'why, then,' I said, 'all is over between us,' I
said, 'and there's others I could mention who worships the
ground I tread on, and wouldn't refuse me nothing,' I said.
And Mr. Simpson, he said ten pounds was a lot of money
and wasn't to be found growing on every bush. So I just
tossed my head and left him, miss; but I shall be seeing him
tomorrow, and then we shall find out if he still thinks the
same."

The next bulletin of Mr. Simpson's state of mind was favorable. After a day of suspense Saunders was able to inform me that all was well.

"I walked out with Mr. Harry Biggs, miss, and Mr. Simpson he met us and he looked so black, and when I saw him
again he said he'd do it, he said. Ho, he is jealous of me,
miss."

Mr. Harry Biggs, I supposed, was the footballer rival.

I slept well that night and dreamed that I was dancing
with Saunders at a house in Belgrave Square, while Mr.
Simpson, who looked exactly like Bob, stood in a corner and
stared at us.


It was a beautiful day on the Monday. I wore my pink
sprigged muslin with a pink sash and the pink chiffon hat
Aunt Edith sent from Paris. Fortunately, the sun was quite
hot, so I was able to have my pink parasol up the whole
time, and words can't express its tremendous duckiness.

The Cave team were practicing when we arrived, and lots of people had come. The Cave man, who was wearing a new Panama, met us at the gate.

"Ah, Sir William," he said, fussing up to father, "you're looking well. Come to knock our bowling about, eh? How do you do, Miss Joan? We're getting quite the young lady now, Sir William, eh? quite the young lady."

"How do you do, Sir Edward?" I said in my number four manner, the distant but gently tolerant. (It wants practice, but I can do it quite well now.)

"I hear you have a new professional this year," said father. "Which is he?"

"Ah, yes, yes; Simpson. You have probably seen his name in the papers. He did well for Sussex last season. There he is, standing by the tent. That tall young fellow."

I eyed Mr. Simpson with interest. He was a nice-looking young man, but gloomy. He was like a man with a secret sorrow. And I don't wonder. I suppose a bowler hates to have to bowl badly on purpose. And there was the ten pounds, too. But he must have thought it worthwhile, or he wouldn't have done it. I could not help wondering what was Saunders's particular attraction. Perhaps I don't see her at her best, reflected over my head in the looking-glass.

Much Middlefold won the toss, and father and another man went in to bat. I was awfully excited. I was afraid, when it actually came to the point, Mr. Simpson's blood would be up to such an extent that he would forget all about Saunders's attractiveness. The other man took the first ball. I could see that he was very much afraid of Mr. Simpson. He looked quite green. He made a huge swipe at the ball and missed it, but it didn't hit the wickets. Then he hit one right into Sir Edward's hands, and Sir Edward let it fall and puffed out his cheeks as if he was annoyed, as I suppose he was. And then Mr. Simpson bowled very fast, and knocked two of the stumps out of the ground.

"It isn't playing the game, don't you know," I heard one of our side say, "bringing a man like Billy Simpson into a country cricket match." He was sitting on the grass not far from me with his pads on. He looked very unhappy. I suppose he was going in to bat soon. "He's too good, don't you know. We shall all be out in half an hour. It spoils all the fun of the thing. They wouldn't like it if we got a lot of first-class pros to come and bat for us. Tell you what—it's a beastly shame!"

The next man missed his first ball; it went past the wicket-keeper. They ran one run, so that now father had to bat against Mr. Simpson.

"If old Romney doesn't do something," said the man who thought Mr. Simpson too good for country cricket, "we're in the cart. He used to be a rattling bat in his time, and he might stop the rot."

He did. I was watching Mr. Simpson very carefully, but I couldn't see that he bowled any differently to father. Still, he must have done, because father hit the ball right into the tent, close to where I was sitting. And the next ball, which was the last of the over, he hit to the boundary again. Everybody clapped hard, and the man sitting on the grass near me said that, if he could keep it up, he would "knock Billy off his length, and then they'd have to have a change."

"And then," said he, "we'll have them on toast."

The match went on in a jerky sort of way. That is to say, father continued to score as if the bowling was the easiest he had ever seen, and the others simply went to the wickets and were instantly destroyed by Mr. Simpson.

"The fact is," said the young man near me, cryptically, "we're all rabbits, and old Romney is the only man on the side who could hit a football." He had himself been in, and been bowled second ball.

The last man was now at the wickets, and it was getting frightfully exciting, for father had made forty-eight. The whole score was only ninety-three. Everybody hoped that the last man would stop in long enough to let father make his fifty—especially myself. I was in such a state of suspense that I dug quite a trench with my parasol. I felt as if I were going to faint.

The other bowler, not Mr. Simpson, was bowling. Father was battling, and he had the whole six balls to make his two runs off.

This bowler had not taken any wickets so far, and I could see that he meant to get father, which would be better than bowling any number of the rabbits, as the young man called them. And father, knowing that he was near his fifty, but not knowing quite how near, was playing very carefully. So it was not till the fifth ball of the over that he managed to make anything, and then it was only one. So now he had made forty-nine. And then that horrid, beastly idiot of a last man went and spooned up the easiest catch, and Sir Edward Cave, of all men, caught it.

I went into a deserted corner and *bellowed*.

Oh, but it was all right after all, because father said that forty-nine not out against one of the best bowlers in England was enough for his simple needs, and that, so far as our bargain was concerned, it should count as fifty.

So I am going to town for the winter, and Mr. Simpson has got his ten-pound note, and will marry Saunders, I suppose, if he hurries and manages it before the football season comes; and father is as pleased as possible with his forty-nine, because he says it restores his faith in himself and relieves him of a haunting fear that he was becoming a veteran; and the entire servants' hall is moaning with envy at Saunders's blue chiffon hat with pink roses.

# The
# Prize Poem

Some quarter of a century before the period with which this story deals, a certain rich and misanthropic man was seized with a bright idea for perpetuating his memory after death, and at the same time harassing a certain section of mankind. So in his will he set aside a portion of his income to be spent on an annual prize for the best poem submitted by a member of the Sixth Form of St. Austin's College, on a subject to be selected by the Headmaster. And, he added—one seems to hear him chuckling to himself—every member of the Form must compete. Then he died. But the evil that men do lives after them, and each year saw a fresh band of unwilling bards goaded to despair by his bequest. True, there were always one or two who hailed this ready market for their sonnets and odes with joy. But the majority, being barely able to rhyme *dove* with *love*, regarded the annual announcement of the subject chosen with feelings of the deepest disgust.

The chains were thrown off after a period of twenty-seven years in this fashion.

Reynolds of the Remove was indirectly the cause of the

change. He was in the infirmary, convalescing after an attack of German measles, when he received a visit from Smith, an ornament of the Sixth.

"By Jove," remarked that gentleman, gazing enviously round the sickroom, "they seem to do you pretty well here."

"Yes, not bad, is it? Take a seat. Anything been happening lately?"

"Nothing much. I suppose you know we beat the M.C.C. by a wicket?"

"Yes, so I heard. Anything else?"

"Prize poem," said Smith, without enthusiasm. He was not a poet.

Reynolds became interested at once. If there was one rôle in which he fancied himself (and, indeed, there were a good many), it was that of versifier. His great ambition was to see some of his lines in print, and he had contracted the habit of sending them up to various periodicals, with no result, so far, except the arrival of rejected MSS. at mealtimes in embarrassingly long envelopes. Which he blushingly concealed with all possible speed.

"What's the subject this year?" he asked.

"The College—of all idiotic things."

"Couldn't have a better subject for an ode. By Jove, I wish I was in the Sixth."

"Wish I was in the infirmary," said Smith.

Reynolds was struck with an idea.

"Look here, Smith," he said, "if you like I'll do you a poem, and you can send it up. If it gets the prize——"

"Oh, it won't get the prize," Smith put in eagerly. "Rogers is a cert for that."

"If it gets the prize," repeated Reynolds, with asperity, "you'll have to tell the Old Man all about it. He'll probably curse a bit, but that can't be helped. How's this for a beginning?

Imposing pile, reared up 'midst pleasant grounds,
   The scene of many a battle, lost or won,
At cricket or at football; whose red walls
   Full many a sun has kissed 'ere day is done.

"Grand. Couldn't you get in something about the M.C.C. match? You could make cricket rhyme with wicket." Smith sat entranced with his ingenuity, but the other treated so material a suggestion with scorn.

"Well," said Smith, "I must be off now. We've got a house match on. Thanks awfully about the poem."

Left to himself, Reynolds set himself seriously to the composing of an ode that should do him justice. That is to say, he drew up a chair and table to the open window, wrote down the lines he had already composed, and began chewing a pen. After a few minutes he wrote another four lines, crossed them out, and selected a fresh piece of paper. He then copied out his first four lines again. After eating his pen to a stump, he jotted down the two words "boys" and "joys" at the end of separate lines. This led him to select a third piece of paper, on which he produced a sort of *edition de luxe* in his best handwriting, with the title "Ode to the College" in printed letters at the top. He was admiring the neat effect of this when the door opened suddenly and violently, and Mrs. Lee, a lady of advanced years and energetic habits, whose duty it was to minister to the needs of the sick and wounded in the infirmary, entered with his tea. Mrs. Lee's method of entering a room was in accordance with the advice of the Psalmist, where he says, "Fling wide the gates." She flung wide the gate of the sickroom, and the result was that what is commonly called "a thorough draught" was established. The air was thick with flying papers, and when calm at length succeeded storm, two editions of an "Ode to the College" were lying on the grass outside.

Reynolds attacked the tea without attempting to retrieve his vanished work. Poetry is good, but tea is better. Besides, he argued within himself, he remembered all he had written, and could easily write it out again. So, as far as he was concerned, those three sheets of paper were a closed book.

Later on in the afternoon, Montgomery of the Sixth happened to be passing by the infirmary, when Fate, aided by a sudden gust of wind, blew a piece of paper at him. "Great Scott," he observed, as his eye fell on the words "Ode to the College." Montgomery, like Smith, was no expert in poetry. He had spent a wretched afternoon trying to hammer out something that would pass muster in the poem competition, but without the least success. There were four lines on the paper. Two more, and it would be a poem, and capable of being entered for the prize as such. The words "imposing pile," with which the fragment in his hand began, took his fancy immensely. A poetic afflatus seized him, and in less than three hours he had added the necessary couplet,

> How truly sweet it is for such as me
> To gaze on thee.

"And dashed neat, too," he said, with satisfaction, as he threw the manuscript into his drawer. "I don't know whether *me* shouldn't be *I,* but they'll have to lump it. It's a poem, anyhow, within the meaning of the act." And he strolled off to a neighbor's study to borrow a book.

Two nights afterwards, Morrison, also of the Sixth, was enjoying his usual during-prep. siesta in his study. A tap at the door roused him. Hastily seizing a lexicon, he assumed the attitude of the seeker after knowledge, and said, "Come in." It was not the Housemaster, but Evans, Morrison's fag, who entered with pride on his face and a piece of paper in his hand.

"I say," he began, "you remember you told me to hunt up some tags for the poem. Will this do?"

Morrison took the paper with a judicial air. On it were the words:

> Imposing pile, reared up 'midst pleasant grounds,
>    The scene of many a battle, lost or won,
> At cricket or at football; whose red walls
>    Full many a sun has kissed ere day was done.

"That's ripping, as far as it goes," said Morrison. "Couldn't be better. You'll find some apples in that box. Better take a few. But look here," with sudden suspicion, "I don't believe you made all this up yourself. Did you?"

Evans finished selecting his apples before venturing on a reply. Then he blushed, as much as a member of the junior school is capable of blushing.

"Well," he said, "I didn't exactly. You see, you only told me to get the tags. You didn't say how."

"But how did you get hold of this? Whose is it?" "Dunno. I found it in the field between the pavilion and the infirmary."

"Oh! well, it doesn't matter much. They're just what I wanted, which is the great thing. Thanks. Shut the door, will you?" Whereupon Evans retired, the richer by many apples, and Morrison resumed his siesta at the point where he had left off.

"Got that poem done yet?" said Smith to Reynolds, pouring out a cup of tea for the invalid on the following Sunday.

"Two lumps, please. No, not quite."

"Great Caesar, man, when'll it be ready, do you think? It's got to go in tomorrow."

"Well, I'm really frightfully sorry, but I got hold of a grand book. Ever read——?"

"Isn't any of it done?" asked Smith.

"Only the first verse. I'm afraid. But, look here, you aren't keen on getting the prize. Why not send in only the one verse? It makes a fairly decent poem."

"Hum! Think the old 'un 'll pass it?"

"He'll have to. There's nothing in the rules about length. Here it is if you want it." "Thanks. I suppose it'll be all right? So long! I must be off."

The Headmaster, known to the world as the Rev. Arthur James Perceval, M.A., and to the school as the old 'un, was sitting at breakfast, stirring his coffee, with a look of marked perplexity upon his dignified face. This was not caused by the coffee, which was excellent, but by a letter which he held in his left hand.

"Hum!" he said. Then "Umph!" in a protesting tone, as if someone had pinched him. Finally, he gave vent to a long-drawn "Um-m-m," in a deep bass. "Most extraordinary. Really, most extraordinary. Exceedingly. Yes. Um. Very." He took a sip of coffee.

"My dear," said he, suddenly. Mrs. Perceval started violently. She had been sketching out in her mind a little dinner, and wondering whether the cook would be equal to it.

"Yes," she said.

"My dear, this is a very extraordinary communication. Exceedingly so. Yes, very."

"Who is it from?"

Mr. Perceval shuddered. He was a purist in speech. *"From whom,* you should say. It is from Mr. Wells, a great college friend of mine. I—ah—submitted to him for examination the poems sent in for the Sixth Form Prize. He writes in a very flippant style. I must say, very flippant. This is his letter:—'Dear Jimmy (really, really, he should remember that we are not so young as we were); dear—ahem—Jimmy. The poems to hand. I have read them, and am writing this from my sickbed. The doctor tells me I may pull through even yet. There was only one any good at all, that was Rogers's, which, though—er—squiffy (tut!) in parts, was a long way better than any of the others. But the most taking part of the whole program was afforded by the three comedians, whose efforts I enclose. You will notice that each begins with exactly the same four lines. Of course, I deprecate cribbing, but you really can't help admiring this sort of thing. There is a reckless daring about it which is simply fascinating. A horrible thought—have they been pulling your dignified leg? By the way, do you remember'—the rest of the letter is—er—on different matters."

"James! How extraordinary!"

"Um, yes. I am reluctant to suspect—er—collusion, but really here there can be no doubt. No doubt at all. No."

"Unless," began Mrs. Perceval, tentatively. "No doubt at all, my dear," snapped Reverend Jimmy. He did not wish to recall the other possibility, that his dignified leg was being pulled.

"Now, for what purpose did I summon you three boys?" asked Mr. Perceval, of Smith, Montgomery, and Morrison, in his room after morning school that day. He generally began a painful interview with this question. The method had distinct advantages. If the criminal were of a nervous disposition, he would give himself away upon the instant. In any case, it was likely to startle him. "For what purpose?" repeated the Headmaster, fixing Smith with a glittering eye.

"I will tell you," continued Mr. Perceval. "It was because I desired information, which none but you can supply. How comes it that each of your compositions for the Poetry Prize commences with the same four lines?" The three poets looked at one another in speechless astonishment.

"Here," he resumed, "are the three papers. Compare them. Now"—after the inspection was over—"what explanation have you to offer. Smith, are these your lines?"

"I-er-ah-*wrote* them, sir."

"Don't prevaricate, Smith. Are you the author of those lines?"

"No, sir."

"Ah! Very good. Are you, Montgomery?"

"No, sir."

"Very good. Then you, Morrison, are exonerated from all blame. You have been exceedingly badly treated. The first-fruit of your brain has been—ah—plucked by others, who toiled not, neither did they spin. You can go, Morrison."

"But, sir——"

"Well, Morrison?"

"I didn't write them, sir."

"I—ah—don't quite understand you, Morrison. You say that you are indebted to another for these lines?"

"Yes, sir."

"To Smith?"

"No, sir."

"To Montgomery?"

"No, sir."

"Then, Morrison, may I ask to whom you are indebted?"

"I found them in the field on a piece of paper, sir." He claimed the discovery himself, because he thought that Evans might possibly prefer to remain outside this tangle.

"So did I, sir." This from Montgomery. Mr. Perceval looked bewildered, as indeed he was.

"And did you, Smith, also find this poem on a piece of paper in the field?" There was a metallic ring of sarcasm in his voice.

"No, sir."

"Ah! Then to what circumstance were you indebted for the lines?"

"I got Reynolds to do them for me, sir."

Montgomery spoke. "It was near the infirmary that I found the paper, and Reynolds is in there."

"So did I, sir," said Morrison, incoherently.

"Then am I to understand, Smith, that to gain the prize you resorted to such underhand means as this?"

"No, sir, we agreed that there was no danger of my getting the prize. If I had got it, I should have told you everything. Reynolds will tell you that, sir."

"Then what object had you in pursuing this deception."

"Well, sir, the rules say everyone must send in something, and I can't write poetry at all, and Reynolds likes it, so I asked him to do it."

And Smith waited for the storm to burst. But it did not burst. Far down in Mr. Perceval's system lurked a quiet sense of humor. The situation penetrated to it. Then he remembered the examiner's letter, and it dawned upon him that there are few crueller things than to make a prosaic person write poetry.

"You may go," he said, and the three went.

And at the next Board Meeting it was decided, mainly owing to the influence of an exceedingly eloquent speech from the Headmaster, to alter the rules for the Sixth Form Poetry Prize, so that from thence onward no one need compete unless he felt himself filled with the immortal fire.

# William Tell
# Told Again

# *Chapter 1*

Once upon a time, more years ago than anybody can remember, before the first hotel had been built or the first Englishman had taken a photograph of Mont Blanc and brought it home to be pasted in an album and shown after tea to his envious friends, Switzerland belonged to the Emperor of Austria, to do what he liked with.

One of the first things the Emperor did was to send his friend Hermann Gessler to govern the country. Gessler was not a nice man, and it soon became plain that he would never make himself really popular with the Swiss. The point on which they disagreed in particular was the question of taxes. The Swiss, who were a simple and thrifty people, objected to paying taxes of any sort. They said they wanted to spend their money on all kinds of other things. Gessler, on the other hand, wished to put a tax on everything, and, being Governor, he did it. He made everyone who owned a flock of sheep pay a certain sum of money to him; and if the farmer sold his sheep and bought cows, he had to pay rather more money to Gessler for the cows than he had paid for the sheep. Gessler also taxed bread, and biscuits, and jam, and buns, and lemonade, and, in fact, everything he could think of, till the people of Switzerland determined to complain. They appointed Walter Fürst, who had red hair and looked fierce; Werner Stauffacher, who had gray hair and was always wondering how he ought to pronounce his name; and Arnold of Melchthal, who had light-yellow hair and was supposed to know a great deal about the law, to make the complaint. They called on the Governor one lovely morning in April, and were shown into the Hall of Audience.

"Well," said Gessler, "and what's the matter now?"

The other two pushed Walter Fürst forward because he looked fierce, and they thought he might frighten the Governor.

Walter Fürst coughed.

"Well?" asked Gessler.

"Er—ahem!" said Walter Fürst.

"That's the way," whispered Werner; *"give* it him!"

"Er—ahem!" said Walter Fürst again; "the fact is, your Governorship——"

"It's a small point," interrupted Gessler, "but I'm generally called 'your Excellency.' Yes?"

"The fact is, your Excellency, it seems to the people of Switzerland——"

"——Whom I represent," whispered Arnold of Melchthal.

"——Whom I represent, that things want changing."

"What things?" inquired Gessler.

"The taxes, your excellent Governorship."

"Change the taxes? Why, don't the people of Switzerland think there are enough taxes?"

Arnold of Melchthal broke in hastily.

"They think there are many too many," he said. "What with the tax on sheep, and the tax on cows, and the tax on bread, and the tax on tea, and the tax——"

"I know, *I* know," Gessler interrupted; "I know all the taxes. Come to the point. What about 'em?"

"Well, your Excellency, there are too many of them."

"Too many!"

"Yes. And we are not going to put up with it any longer!" shouted Arnold of Melchthal.

Gessler leaned forward in his throne.

"Might I ask you to repeat that remark?" he said.

"We are not going to put up with it any longer!"

Gessler sat back again with an ugly smile.

"Oh," he said—"oh, indeed! You aren't, aren't you! Desire the Lord High Executioner to step this way," he added to a soldier who stood beside him.

The Lord High Executioner entered the presence. He was a kind-looking old gentleman with white hair, and he wore a beautiful black robe, tastefully decorated with death's heads.

"Your Excellency sent for me?" he said.

"Just so," replied Gessler. "This gentleman here"—he pointed to Arnold of Melchthal—"says he does not like taxes, and that he isn't going to put up with them any longer."

"Tut-tut!" murmured the executioner.

"See what you can do for him."

"Certainly, your Excellency. Robert," he cried, "is the oil on the boil?"

"Just this minute boiled over," replied a voice from the other side of the door.

"Then bring it in, and mind you don't spill any."

Enter Robert, in a suit of armor and a black mask, carrying a large caldron, from which the steam rose in great clouds.

"Now, sir, if you please," said the executioner politely to Arnold of Melchthal.

Arnold looked at the caldron.

"Why, it's hot," he said.

"Warmish," admitted the executioner.

"It's against the law to threaten a man with hot oil."

"You may bring an action against me," said the executioner. "Now, sir, if *you* please. We are wasting time. The forefinger of your left hand, if I may trouble you. Thank you. I am obliged."

He took Arnold's left hand, and dipped the tip of the first finger into the oil.

"Ow!" cried Arnold, jumping.

"Don't let him see he's hurting you," whispered Werner Stauffacher. "Pretend you don't notice it."

Gessler leaned forward again.

"Have your views on taxes changed at all?" he asked. "Do you see my point of view more clearly now?"

Arnold admitted that he thought that, after all, there might be something to be said for it.

"That's right," said the Governor. "And the tax on sheep? You don't object to that?"

"No."

"And the tax on cows?"

"I like it."

"And those on bread, and buns, and lemonade?"

"I enjoy them."

"Excellent. In fact, you're quite contented?"

"Quite."

"And you think the rest of the people are?"

"Oh, quite, quite!"

"And do you think the same?" he asked of Walter and Werner.

"Oh *yes*, your Excellency!" they cried.

"Then *that's* all right," said Gessler. "I was sure you would be sensible about it. Now, if you will kindly place in the tambourine which the gentleman on my left is presenting to you a mere trifle to compensate us for our trouble in giving you

an audience, and if you" (to Arnold of Melchthal) "will con-
tribute an additional trifle for use of the Imperial boiling oil,
I think we shall all be satisfied. You've done it? *That's* right.
Good-bye, and mind the step as you go out."

And, as he finished this speech, the three spokesmen of
the people of Switzerland were shown out of the Hall of Audience.

## *Chapter 2*

They were met in the street outside by a large body of their
fellow citizens, who had accompanied them to the Palace,
and who had been spending the time since their departure
in listening by turns at the keyhole of the front door. But as
the Hall of Audience was at the other side of the Palace, and
cut off from the front door by two other doors, a flight of
stairs, and a long passage, they had not heard very much of
what had gone on inside, and they surrounded the three
spokesmen as they came out, and questioned them eagerly.

"Has he taken off the tax on jam?" asked Ulric the smith.

"What is he going to do about the tax on mixed biscuits?"
shouted Klaus von der Flue, who was a chimney sweep of
the town and loved mixed biscuits.

"Never mind about tea and mixed biscuits!" cried his
neighbor, Meier of Sarnen. "What I want to know is whether
we shall have to pay for keeping sheep any more."

"What *did* the Governor say?" asked Jost Weiler, a practical man, who liked to go straight to the point.

The three spokesmen looked at one another a little doubt-
fully.

"We-e-ll," said Werner Stauffacher at last, "as a matter of
fact, he didn't actually *say* very much. It was more what he
*did,* if you understand me, than what he said."

"I should describe His Excellency the Governor," said Walter Fürst, "as a man who has got a way with him—a man who has got all sorts of arguments at his fingertips."

At the mention of fingertips, Arnold of Melchthal uttered a sharp howl.

"In short," continued Walter, "after a few minutes' very interesting conversation he made us see that it really wouldn't do, and that we must go on paying the taxes as before."

There was a dead silence for several minutes, while everybody looked at everybody else in dismay.

The silence was broken by Arnold of Sewa. Arnold of Sewa had been disappointed at not being chosen as one of the three spokesmen, and he thought that if he had been so chosen all this trouble would not have occurred.

"The fact is," he said bitterly, "that you three have failed to do what you were sent to do. I mention no names—far from it—but I don't mind saying that there are some people in this town who would have given a better account of themselves. What you want in little matters of this sort is, if I may say so, tact. Tact; that's what you want. Of course, if you *will* go rushing into the Governor's presence——"

"But we didn't rush," said Walter Fürst.

"——Shouting out that you want the taxes abolished——"

"But we didn't shout," said Walter Fürst.

"I really cannot speak if I am to be constantly interrupted," said Arnold of Sewa severely. "What I say is, that you ought to employ tact. Tact; that's what you want. If I had been chosen to represent the Swiss people in this affair—I am not saying I ought to have been, mind you; I merely say *if* I had been—I should have acted rather after the following fashion: Walking firmly, but not defiantly, into the tyrant's presence, I should have broken the ice with some pleasant remark about the weather. The conversation once started, the rest would have been easy. I should have said that I hoped His Excellency had enjoyed a good dinner. Once on the subject of food, and it would have been the simplest of tasks to show him how unnecessary taxes on food were, and the whole affair would have been pleasantly settled while you waited. I do not imply that the Swiss people would have done better to have chosen me as their representative. I merely say that that is how I should have acted had they done so."

And Arnold of Sewa twirled his moustache and looked offended. His friends instantly suggested that he should be allowed to try where the other three had failed, and the rest of the crowd, beginning to hope once more, took up the cry. The result was that the visitors' bell of the Palace was rung for the second time. Arnold of Sewa went in, and the door was banged behind him.

Five minutes later he came out, sucking the first finger of his left hand.

"No," he said, "it can't be done. The tyrant has convinced me."

"I knew he would," said Arnold of Melchthal.

"Then I think you might have warned me," snapped Arnold of Sewa, dancing with the pain of his burnt finger.

"Was it hot?"

"Boiling."

"Ah!"

"Then he really won't let us off the taxes?" asked the crowd in disappointed voices.

"No."

"Then the long and short of it is," said Walter Fürst, drawing a deep breath, "that we must rebel!"

"Rebel?" cried everybody.

"Rebel!" repeated Walter firmly.

"We will!" cried everybody.

"Down with the tyrant!" shouted Walter Fürst.

"Down with the taxes!" shrieked the crowd.

A scene of great enthusiasm followed. The last words were spoken by Werner Stauffacher.

"We want a leader," he said.

"I don't wish to thrust myself forward," began Arnold of Sewa, "but I must say, if it comes to leading——"

"And I know the very man for the job," said Werner Stauffacher. "William Tell!"

"Hurrah for William Tell!" roared the crowd, and, taking the time from Werner Stauffacher, they burst into the grand old Swiss chant which runs as follows:

> For he's a jolly good fellow!
> For he's a jolly good fellow!!
> For he's a jolly good fe-e-ll-ow!!!!
> And so say all of us!

And having sung this till they were all quite hoarse, they went off to their beds to get a few hours' sleep before beginning the labors of the day.

## Chapter 3

In a picturesque little châlet high up in the mountains, covered with snow and edelweiss (which is a flower that grows in the Alps, and you are not allowed to pick it), dwelt William Tell, his wife Hedwig, and his two sons, Walter and William. Such a remarkable man was Tell that I think I must devote a whole chapter to him and his exploits. There was really nothing he could not do. He was the best shot with the crossbow in the whole of Switzerland. He had the courage of a lion, the sure footedness of a wild goat, the agility of a squirrel, and a beautiful beard. If you wanted someone to hurry across desolate ice fields, and leap from crag to crag after a chamois, Tell was the man for your money. If you wanted a man to say rude things to the Governor, it was to Tell that you applied first. Once when he was hunting in the wild ravine of Schächenthal, where men were hardly ever to be seen, he met the Governor face to face. There was no way of getting past. On one side the rocky wall rose sheer up, while below the river roared. Directly Gessler caught sight of Tell striding along with his crossbow, his cheeks grew pale and his knees tottered, and he sat down on a rock feeling very unwell indeed.

"Aha!" said Tell. "Oho! so it's you, is it? *I* know you. And a nice sort of person you are, with your taxes on bread and sheep, aren't you! You'll come to a bad end one of these days, that's what will happen to you. Oh, you old reprobate! Pooh!" And he had passed on with a look of scorn, leaving Gessler to think over what he had said. And Gessler ever since had had a grudge against him, and was only waiting for a chance of paying him out.

"Mark my words," said Tell's wife, Hedwig, when her husband told her about it after supper that night—"mark my words, he will never forgive you."

"I will avoid him," said Tell. "He will not seek me."

"Well, mind you do," was Hedwig's reply.

On another occasion, when the Governor's soldiers were chasing a friend of his, called Baumgarten, and when Baumgarten's only chance of escape was to cross the lake during a fierce storm, and when the ferryman, sensibly remarking, "What! must I rush into the jaws of death? No man that hath his senses would do that!" refused to take out his boat even for twice his proper fare, and when the soldiers rode down to seize their prey with dreadful shouts, Tell jumped into the boat, and, rowing with all his might, brought his friend safe across after a choppy passage. Which made Gessler the Governor still more angry with him.

But it was as a marksman that Tell was so extraordinary. There was nobody in the whole of the land who was half so skillful. He attended every meeting for miles around where there was a shooting competition, and every time he won first prize. Even his rivals could not help praising his skill. "Behold!" they would say, "Tell is quite the pot-hunter," meaning by the last word a man who always went in for every prize, and always won it. And Tell would say, "Yes, truly am I a pot-hunter, for I hunt to fill the family pot." And so he did. He never came home empty-handed from the chase. Sometimes it was a chamois that he brought back, and then the family had it roasted on the first day, cold on the next four, and minced on the sixth, with sippets of toast round the edge of the dish. Sometimes it was only a bird and then Hedwig would say, "Mark my words, this fowl will not go round." But it always did, and it never happened that there was not even a fowl to eat.

In fact, Tell and his family lived a very happy, contented life, in spite of the Governor Gessler and his taxes.

Tell was very patriotic. He always believed that some day the Swiss would rise and rebel against the tyranny of the Governor, and he used to drill his two children so as to keep them always in a state of preparation. They would march about, beating tin cans and shouting, and altogether enjoying themselves immensely, though Hedwig, who did not like noise, and wanted Walter and William to help her with the housework, made frequent complaints. "Mark my words," she would say, "this growing spirit of militarism in the young and foolish will lead to no good," meaning that boys who played at soldiers instead of helping their mother to dust the chairs and scrub the kitchen floor would in all probability come to a bad end. But Tell would say, "Who hopes to fight his way through life must be prepared to wield arms. Carry on, my boys!" And they carried on. It was to this man that the Swiss people had determined to come for help.

# Chapter 4

Talking matters over in the inn of the town, the "Glass and Glacier", the citizens came to the conclusion that they ought to appoint three spokesmen to go and explain to Tell just what they wanted him to do.

"I don't wish to seem to boast at all," said Arnold of Sewa, "but I think I had better be one of the three."

"I was thinking," said Werner Stauffacher, "that it would be a pity always to be chopping and changing. Why not choose the same three as were sent to Gessler?"

"I don't desire to be unpleasant at all," replied Arnold of Sewa, "but I must be forgiven for reminding the honorable gentleman who has just spoken that he and his equally honorable friends did not meet with the best of success when they called upon the Governor."

"Well, and you didn't either!" snapped Arnold of Melchthal, whose finger still hurt him, and made him a little bad tempered.

"That," said Arnold of Sewa, "I put down entirely to the fact that you and your friends, by not exercising tact, irritated the Governor, and made him unwilling to listen to anybody else. Nothing is more important in these affairs than tact. That's what you want—tact. But have it your own way. Don't mind *me!*"

And the citizens did not. They chose Werner Stauffacher, Arnold of Melchthal, and Walter Fürst, and, having drained their glasses, the three trudged up the steep hill which led to Tell's house.

It had been agreed that everyone should wait at the "Glass and Glacier" until the three spokesmen returned, in order that they might hear the result of their mission. Everybody was very anxious. A revolution without Tell would be quite impossible, and it was not unlikely that Tell might refuse to be their leader. The worst of a revolution is that, if it fails, the leader is always executed as an example to the rest. And many people object to being executed, however much it may set a good example to their friends. On the other hand, Tell was a brave man and a patriot, and might be only too eager to try to throw off the tyrant's yoke, whatever the risk. They had waited about an hour, when they saw the three spokesmen coming down the hill. Tell was not with them, a fact which made the citizens suspect that he had refused their offer. The first thing a man does when he has accepted the leadership of a revolution is to come and plot with his companions.

"Well?" said everybody eagerly, as the three arrived.

Werner Stauffacher shook his head.

"Ah," said Arnold of Sewa, "I see what it is. He has refused. You didn't exercise tact, and he refused."

"We *did* exercise tact," said Stauffacher indignantly; "but he would not be persuaded. It was like this: We went to the house and knocked at the door. Tell opened it. 'Good-morning,' I said.

" 'Good-morning,' said he. 'Take a seat.'

"I took a seat.

" 'My heart is full,' I said, 'and longs to speak with you.' I thought that a neat way of putting it."

The company murmured approval.

" 'A heavy heart,' said Tell, 'will not grow light with words.' "

"Not bad that!" murmured Jost Weiler. "Clever way of putting things, Tell has got."

" 'Yet words,' I said, 'might lead us on to deeds.' "

"Neat," said Jost Weiler—"very neat. Yes?"

"To which Tell's extraordinary reply was: 'The only thing to do is to sit still.'

" 'What!' I said; 'bear in silence things unbearable?'

" 'Yes,' said Tell; 'to peaceable men peace is gladly

granted. When the Governor finds that his oppression does not make us revolt, he will grow tired of oppressing.' "

"And what did you say to that?" asked Ulric the smith.

"I said he did not know the Governor if he thought he could ever grow tired of oppressing. 'We might do much,' I said, 'if we held fast together. Union is strength,' I said.

" 'The strong,' said Tell, 'is the strongest when he stands alone.'

" 'Then our country must not count on thee,' I said, 'when in despair she stands on self-defence?'

" 'Oh, well,' he said, 'hardly that, perhaps. I don't want to desert you. What I mean to say is, I'm no use as a plotter or a counselor and that sort of thing. Where I come out strong is in deeds. So don't invite me to your meetings and make me speak, and that sort of thing; but if you want a man to *do* anything—why, that's where I shall come in, you see. Just write if you want me—a postcard will do—and you will not find William Tell hanging back. No, sir.' And with those words he showed us out."

"Well," said Jost Weiler, "I call that encouraging. All we have to do now is to plot. Let us plot."

"Yes, let's!" shouted everybody.

Ulric the smith rapped for silence on the table.

"Gentlemen," he said, "our friend Mr. Klaus von der Flue will now read a paper on 'Governors—their drawbacks, and how to get rid of them.' Silence, gentlemen, please. Now, then, Klaus, old fellow, speak up and get it over."

And the citizens settled down without further delay to a little serious plotting.

# Chapter 5

A few days after this, Hedwig gave Tell a good talking to on the subject of his love for adventure. He was sitting at the door of his house mending an axe. Hedwig, as usual, was washing up. Walter and William were playing with a little crossbow not far off.

"Father," said Walter.

"Yes, my boy?"

"My bowstrong has bust." ("Bust" was what all Swiss boys said when they meant "broken.")

"You must mend it yourself, my boy," said Tell. "A sportsman always helps himself."

"What *I* say," said Hedwig, bustling out of the house, "is that a boy of his age has no business to be shooting. I don't like it."

"Nobody can shoot well if he does not begin to practice early. Why, when I was a boy—I remember on one occasion, when——"

"What *I* say," interrupted Hedwig, "is that a boy ought not to want always to be shooting, and what not. He ought to stay at home and help his mother. And I wish you would set them a better example."

"Well, the fact is, you know," said Tell, "I don't think Nature meant me to be a stay-at-home and that sort of thing. I couldn't be a herdsman if you paid me. I shouldn't know what to do. No, everyone has his special line, and mine is hunting. Now, I *can* hunt."

"A nasty, dangerous occupation," said Hedwig. "I don't like to hear of your being lost on desolate ice fields, and leaping from crag to crag, and what not. Some day, mark my words, if you are not careful, you will fall down a precipice, or be overtaken by an avalanche, or the ice will break while you are crossing it. There are a thousand ways in which you might get hurt."

"A man of ready wit with a quick eye," replied Tell complacently, "never gets hurt. The mountain has no terror for her children. I am a child of the mountain."

"You are certainly a child!" snapped Hedwig. "It is no use my arguing with you."

"Not very much," agreed Tell, "for I am just off to the town. I have an appointment with your papa and some other gentlemen."

(I forgot to say so before, but Hedwig was the daughter of Walter Fürst.)

"Now, *what* are you and papa plotting?" asked Hedwig. "I know there is something going on. I suspected it when papa brought Werner Stauffacher and the other man here, and you wouldn't let me listen. What is it? Some dangerous scheme, I suppose?"

"Now, how in the world do you get those sort of ideas into your head?" Tell laughed. "Dangerous scheme! As if I should plot dangerous schemes with your papa!"

"*I* know," said Hedwig. "You can't deceive *me!* There is a plot afoot against the Governor, and you are in it."

"A man must help his country."

"They're sure to place you where there is most danger. I know them. Don't go. Send Walter down with a note to say that you regret that an unfortunate previous engagement, which you have just recollected, will make it impossible for you to accept their kind invitation to plot."

"No; I must go."

"And there is another thing," continued Hedwig, "Gessler the Governor is in the town now."

"He goes away today."

"Well, wait till he has gone. You must not meet him. He bears you malice."

"To me his malice cannot do much harm. I do what's right, and fear no enemy."

"Those who do right," said Hedwig, "are those he hates

the most. And you know he has never forgiven you for speaking like that when you met him in the ravine. Keep away from the town for today. Do anything else. Go hunting, if you will."

"No," said Tell; "I promised. I must go. Come along, Walter."

"You *aren't* going to take that poor *dear* child? Come here, Walter, directly this minute!"

"Want to go with father," said Walter, beginning to cry, for his father had promised to take him with him the next time he went to the town, and he had saved his pocket money for the occasion.

"Oh, let the boy come," said Tell. "William will stay with you, won't you, William?"

"All right, father," said William.

"Well, mark my words," said Hedwig, "if something bad does not happen I shall be surprised."

"Oh no," said Tell. "What can happen?"

And without further delay he set off with Walter for the town.

# Chapter 6

In the meantime all kinds of things of which Tell had no suspicion had been happening in the town. The fact that there were no newspapers in Switzerland at that time often made him a little behindhand as regarded the latest events. He had to depend, as a rule, on visits from his friends, who would sit in his kitchen and tell him all about everything that had been going on for the last few days. And, of course, when there was anything very exciting happening in the town, nobody had time to trudge up the hill to Tell's châlet. They all wanted to be in the town enjoying the fun.

What had happened now was this. It was the chief amusement of the Governor, Gessler (who, you will remember, was *not* a nice man), when he had a few moments to spare from the cares of governing, to sit down and think out some new way of annoying the Swiss people. He was one of those persons who

> only do it to annoy,
> Because they know it teases.

What he liked chiefly was to forbid something. He would find out what the people most enjoyed doing, and then he would send a herald to say that he was very sorry, but it must stop. He found that this annoyed the Swiss more than anything. But now he was rather puzzled what to do, for he had forbidden everything he could think of. He had forbidden dancing and singing, and playing on any sort of musical instrument, on the ground that these things made such a noise, and disturbed people who wanted to work. He had forbidden the eating of everything except bread and the simplest sorts of meat, because he said that anything else upset people, and made them unfit to do anything except sit still and say how ill they were. And he had forbidden all sorts of games, because he said they were a waste of time.

So that now, though he wanted dreadfully to forbid something else, he could not think of anything.

Then he had an idea, and this was it:

He told his servants to cut a long pole. And they cut a very long pole. Then he said to them, "Go into the hall and bring me one of my hats. Not my best hat, which I wear on Sundays and on State occasions; nor yet my second-best, which I wear every day; nor yet, again, the one I wear when I am out hunting, for all these I need. Fetch me, rather, the oldest of my hats." And they fetched him the very oldest of his hats. Then he said, "Put it on top of the pole." And they put it right on top of the pole. And, last of all, he said, "Go and set up the pole in the middle of the meadow just outside the gates of the town." And they went and set up the pole in the very middle of the meadow just outside the gates of the town.

Then he sent his heralds out to north and south and east and west to summon the people together, because he said he had something very important and special to say to them. And the people came in tens, and fifties, and hundreds, men, women, and children; and they stood waiting in front of the Palace steps till Gessler the Governor should come out and say something very important and special to them.

And punctually at eleven o'clock, Gessler, having finished a capital breakfast, came out on to the top step and spoke to them.

"Ladies and gentlemen,"——he began. (A voice from the crowd: "Speak up!")

"Ladies and gentlemen," he began again, in a louder voice, "if I could catch the man who said 'Speak up!' I would have him bitten in the neck by wild elephants. (Applause.) I have called you to this place today to explain to you my reason for putting up a pole, on the top of which is one of my caps, in the meadow just outside the city gates. It is this: You all, I know, respect and love me." Here he paused for the audience to cheer, but as they remained quite silent he went on: "You would all, I know, like to come to my Palace every day and do reverence to me. (A voice: 'No, no!') If I could catch the man who said 'No, no!' I would have him stung on the soles of the feet by pink scorpions; and if he was the same man who said 'Speak up!' a little while ago, the number of scorpions should be doubled. (Loud applause.) As I was saying before I was interrupted, I know you would like to come to my Palace and do reverence to me there. But, as you are many and space is limited, I am obliged to refuse you that pleasure. However, being anxious not to disappoint you, I have set up my cap in the meadow, and you may do reverence to *that*. In fact, you *must*. Everybody is to look on that cap as if it were me. (A voice: 'It ain't so ugly as you!') If I could catch the man who made that remark I would have him tied up and teased by trained bluebottles. (Deafening applause.) In fact, to put the matter briefly, if anybody crosses that meadow without bowing down before that cap, my soldiers will arrest him, and I will have him pecked on the nose by infuriated blackbirds. So there! Soldiers, move that crowd on!"

And Gessler disappeared indoors again, just as a volley of eggs and cabbages whistled through the air. And the soldiers began to hustle the crowd down the various streets till the open space in front of the Palace gates was quite cleared of them. All this happened the day before Tell and Walter set out for the town.

## *Chapter 7*

Having set up the pole and cap in the meadow, Gessler sent two of his bodyguard, Friesshardt (I should think you would be safe in pronouncing this Freeze-hard, but you had better ask somebody who knows) and Leuthold, to keep watch there all day, and see that nobody passed by without kneeling down before the pole and taking off his hat to it.

But the people, who prided themselves on being what they called *üppen zie schnuffen*, or, as we should say, "up to snuff," and equal to every occasion, had already seen a way out of the difficulty. They knew that if they crossed the meadow they must bow down before the pole, which they did not want to do, so it occurred to them that an ingenious way of preventing this would be not to cross the meadow. So they went the long way round, and the two soldiers spent a lonely day.

"What I sez," said Friesshardt, "is, wot's the use of us wasting our time here?" (Friesshardt was not a very well-educated man, and he did not speak good grammar.) "None of these here people ain't a-going to bow down to that there hat. Of course they ain't. Why, I can remember the time when this meadow was like a fair—everybody a-shoving and a-jostling one another for elbow room; and look at it now! It's a desert. That's what it is, a desert. What's the good of us wasting of our time here, I sez. That's what I sez.

"And they're artful, too, mind yer," he continued. "Why, only this morning, I sez to myself, 'Friesshardt,' I sez, 'you just wait till twelve o'clock,' I sez, ' 'cos that's when they leave the council house, and then they'll *have* to cross the meadow. And then we'll see what we *shall* see,' I sez. Like that, I sez. Bitterlike, yer know. 'We'll see,' I sez, 'what we *shall* see.' So I waited, and at twelve o'clock out they came, dozens of them, and began to cross the meadow. 'And now,' sez I to myself, 'look out for larks.' But what happened? Why, when they came to the pole, the priest stood in front of it, and the sacristan rang the bell, and they all fell down on their knees. But they were saying their prayers, not doing obeisance to the hat. That's what *they* were doing. Artful—that's what *they* are!"

And Friesshardt kicked the foot of the pole viciously with his iron boot.

"It's my belief," said Leuthold—"it's my firm belief that they are laughing at us. There! Listen to that!"

A voice made itself heard from behind a rock not far off.

"Where did you get that hat?" said the voice.

"There!" grumbled Leuthold; "they're always at it. Last time it was, 'Who's your hatter?' Why, we're the laughing-stock of the place. We're like two rogues in a pillory. 'Tis rank disgrace for one who wears a sword to stand as sentry o'er an empty hat. To make obeisance to a hat! I' faith, such a command is downright foolery!"

"Well," said Friesshardt, "and why not bow before an empty hat? Thou hast oft bow'd before an empty skull. Ha, ha! I was always one for a joke, yer know."

"Here come some people," said Leuthold. "At last! And they're only the rabble, after all. You don't catch any of the better sort of people coming here."

A crowd was beginning to collect on the edge of the meadow. Its numbers swelled every minute, until quite a hundred of the commoner sort must have been gathered together. They stood pointing at the pole and talking among themselves, but nobody made any movement to cross the meadow.

At last somebody shouted "Yah!"

The soldiers took no notice.

Somebody else cried "Booh!"

"Pass along there, pass along!" said the soldiers.

Cries of "Where did you get that hat?" began to come from the body of the crowd. When the Swiss invented a catch phrase they did not drop it in a hurry.

"Where—did—you—get—that—HAT?" they shouted.

Friesshardt and Leuthold stood like two statues in armor, paying no attention to the remarks of the rabble. This annoyed the rabble. They began to be more personal.

"You in the second-hand lobster-tin," shouted one—he meant Friesshardt, whose suit of armor, though no longer new, hardly deserved this description—"who's your hatter?"

"Can't yer see," shouted a friend, when Friesshardt made no reply, "the pore thing ain't alive? 'E's stuffed!"

Roars of laughter greeted this sally. Friesshardt, in spite of the fact that he enjoyed a joke, turned pink.

" 'E's blushing!" shrieked a voice.

Friesshardt turned purple.

Then things got still more exciting.

" 'Ere," said a rough voice in the crowd impatiently, "wot's the good of *torkin'* to 'em? Gimme that 'ere egg, missus!"

And in another instant an egg flew across the meadow, and burst over Leuthold's shoulder. The crowd howled with delight. This was something *like* fun, thought they, and the next moment eggs, cabbages, cats, and missiles of every sort darkened the air. The two soldiers raved and shouted, but did not dare to leave their post. At last, just as the storm was at its height, it ceased, as if by magic. Everyone in the crowd turned round, and, as he turned, jumped into the air and waved his hat.

A deafening cheer went up.

"Hurrah!" cried the mob; "here comes good old Tell! *Now* there's going to be a jolly row!"


## Chapter 8

Tell came striding along, Walter by his side, and his crossbow over his shoulder. He knew nothing about the hat having been placed on the pole, and he was surprised to see such a large crowd gathered in the meadow. He bowed to the crowd in his polite way, and the crowd gave three cheers and one more, and he bowed again.

"Hullo!" said Walter suddenly; "look at that hat up there, father. On the pole."

"What is the hat to us?" said Tell, and he began to walk across the meadow with an air of great dignity, and Walter walked by his side, trying to look just like him.

"Here! hi!" shouted the soldiers. "Stop! You haven't bowed down to the cap."

Tell looked scornful, but said nothing. Walter looked still more scornful.

"Ho, there!" shouted Friesshardt, standing in front of him. "I bid you stand in the Emperor's name."

"My good fellow," said Tell, "please do not bother me. I am in a hurry. I really have nothing for you."

"My orders is," said Friesshardt, "to stand in this 'ere meadow and to see as how all them what passes through it does obeisance to that there hat. Them's Governor's orders, them is. So now."

"My good fellow," said Tell, "let me pass. I shall get cross, I know I shall."

Shouts of encouragement from the crowd, who were waiting patiently for the trouble to begin.

"Go it, Tell!" they cried. "Don't stand talking to him. Hit him a kick!"

Friesshardt became angrier every minute.

"My orders is," he said again, "to arrest them as don't bow down to the hat, and for two pins, young feller, I'll arrest you. So which is it to be? Either you bow down to that there hat or you come along of me."

Tell pushed him aside, and walked on with his chin in the air. Walter went with him, with *his* chin in the air.

WHACK!

A howl of dismay went up from the crowd as they saw Friesshardt raise his pike and bring it down with all his force on Tell's head. The sound of the blow went echoing through the meadow and up the hills and down the valleys.

"Ow!" cried Tell.

"*Now,*" thought the crowd, "things must begin to get exciting."

Tell's first idea was that one of the larger mountains in the neighborhood had fallen on top of him. Then he thought that there must have been an earthquake. Then it gradually dawned upon him that he had been hit by a mere common soldier with a pike. Then he *was* angry.

"Look here!" he began.

"Look there!" said Friesshardt, pointing to the cap.

"You've hurt my head very much," said Tell. "Feel the bump. If I hadn't happened to have a particularly hard head I don't know what might not have happened," and he raised his fist and hit Friesshardt; but as Friesshardt was wearing a thick iron helmet the blow did not hurt him very much.

But it had the effect of bringing the crowd to Tell's assistance. They had been waiting all this time for him to begin the fighting, for though they were very anxious to attack the soldiers, they did not like to do so by themselves. They wanted a leader.

So when they saw Tell hit Friesshardt, they tucked up their sleeves, grasped their sticks and cudgels more tightly, and began to run across the meadow towards him.

Neither of the soldiers noticed this. Friesshardt was busy arguing with Tell, and Leuthold was laughing at Friesshardt. So when the people came swarming up with their sticks and cudgels they were taken by surprise. But every soldier in the service of Gessler was as brave as a lion, and Friesshardt and Leuthold were soon hitting back merrily, and making a good many of the crowd wish that they had stayed at home. The two soldiers were wearing armor, of course, so that it was difficult to hurt them; but the crowd, who wore no armor, found that *they* could get hurt very easily. Conrad Hunn, for instance, was attacking Friesshardt, when the soldier happened to drop his pike. It fell on Conrad's toe, and Conrad limped away, feeling that fighting was no fun unless you had thick boots on.

And so for a time the soldiers had the best of the fight.

## Chapter 9

For many minutes the fight raged furiously round the pole, and the earth shook beneath the iron boots of Friesshardt and Leuthold as they rushed about, striking out right and left with their fists and the flats of their pikes. Seppi the cowboy (an ancestor, by the way, of Buffalo Bill) went down before a tremendous blow by Friesshardt, and Leuthold knocked Klaus von der Flue head over heels.

"What you *want*," said Arnold of Sewa, who had seen the beginning of the fight from the window of his cottage and had hurried to join it, and as usual, to give advice to everybody—"what you want here is guile. That's what you want—guile, cunning. Not brute force, mind you. It's no good rushing at a man in armor and hitting him. He only hits you back. You should employ guile. Thus. Observe."

He had said these words standing on the outskirts of the crowd. He now grasped his cudgel and began to steal slowly towards Friesshardt, who had just given Werni the huntsman such a hit with his pike that the sound of it was still echoing in the mountains, and was now busily engaged in disposing of Jost Weiler. Arnold of Sewa crept stealthily behind him, and was just about to bring his cudgel down on his head, when Leuthold, catching sight of him, saved his comrade by driving his pike with all his force into Arnold's side. Arnold said afterwards that it completely took his breath away. He rolled over, and after being trodden on by everybody for some minutes, got up and limped back to his cottage, where he went straight to bed, and did not get up for two days.

All this time Tell had been standing a little way off with his arms folded, looking on. While it was a quarrel simply between himself and Friesshardt he did not mind fighting. But when the crowd joined in he felt that it was not fair to help so many men attack one, however badly that one might have behaved.

He now saw the the time had come to put an end to the disturbance. He drew an arrow from his quiver, placed it in his crossbow, and pointed it at the hat. Friesshardt, seeing what he intended to do, uttered a shout of horror and rushed to stop him. But at that moment somebody in the crowd hit him so hard with a spade that his helmet was knocked over his eyes, and before he could raise it again the deed was done. Through the cap and through the pole and out at the other side sped the arrow. And the first thing he saw when he opened his eyes was Tell standing beside him twirling his moustache, while all around the crowd danced and shouted and threw their caps into the air with joy.

"A mere trifle," said Tell modestly.

The crowd cheered again and again.

Friesshardt and Leuthold lay on the ground beside the pole, feeling very sore and bruised, and thought that perhaps, on the whole, they had better stay there. There was no knowing what the crowd might do after this, if they began to fight again. So they lay on the ground and made no attempt to interfere with the popular rejoicings. What they *wanted,* as Arnold of Sewa might have said if he had been there, was a few moments complete rest. Leuthold's helmet had been hammered with sticks until it was over his eyes and all out of shape, and Friesshardt's was very little better. And they both felt just as if they had been run over in the street by a horse and cart.

"Tell!" shouted the crowd. "Hurrah for Tell! Good old Tell!"

"Tell's the boy!" roared Ulric the smith. "Not another man in Switzerland could have made that shot."

"No," shrieked everybody, "not another!"

"Speech!" cried someone from the edge of the crowd.

"Speech! Speech! Tell, speech!" Everybody took up the cry.

"No, no," said Tell, blushing.

"Go on, go on!" shouted the crowd.

"Oh, I couldn't," said Tell; "I don't know what to say."

"Anything will do. Speech! Speech!"

Ulric the smith and Ruodi the fisherman hoisted Tell on to their shoulders, and, having coughed once or twice, he said:

"Gentlemen——"

Cheers from the crowd.

"Gentlemen," said Tell again, "this is the proudest moment of my life."

More cheers.

"I don't know what you want me to talk about. I have never made a speech before. Excuse my emotion. This is the proudest moment of my life. Today is a great day for Switzerland. We have struck the first blow of the revolution. Let us strike some more."

Shouts of "Hear, hear!" from the crowd, many of whom, misunderstanding Tell's last remark, proceeded to hit Leuthold and Friesshardt, until stopped by cries of "Order!" from Ulric the smith.

"Gentlemen," continued Tell, "the floodgates of revolution have been opened. From this day they will stalk through the land burning to ashes the slough of oppression which our tyrant Governor has erected in our midst. I have only to add that this is the proudest moment of my life, and——"

He was interrupted by a frightened voice.

"Look out, you chaps," said the voice; "here comes the Governor!"

Gessler, with a bodyguard of armed men, had entered the meadow, and was galloping towards them.

# Chapter 10

Gessler came riding up on his brown horse, and the crowd melted away in all directions, for there was no knowing what the Governor might not do if he found them plotting. They were determined to rebel and to throw off his tyrannous yoke, but they preferred to do it quietly and comfortably, when he was nowhere near.

So they ran away to the edge of the meadow, and stood there in groups, waiting to see what was going to happen. Not even Ulric the smith and Ruodi the fisherman waited, though they knew quiet well that Tell had not nearly finished his speech. They set the orator down, and began to walk away, trying to look as if they had been doing nothing in particular, and were going to go on doing it—only somewhere else.

Tell was left standing alone in the middle of the meadow by the pole. He scorned to run away like the others, but he did not at all like the look of things. Gessler was a stern man, quick to punish any insult, and there were two of his soldiers lying on the ground with their nice armor all spoiled and dented, and his own cap on top of the pole had an arrow right through the middle of it, and would never look the same again, however much it might be patched. It seemed to Tell that there was a bad time coming.

Gessler rode up, and reined in his horse.

"Now then, now then, now then!" he said, in his quick, abrupt way. "What's this? what's this? what's this?"

(When a man repeats what he says three times, you can see that he is not in a good temper.)

Friesshardt and Leuthold got up, saluted, and limped slowly towards him. They halted beside his horse, and stood to attention. The tears trickled down their cheeks.

"Come, come, come!" said Gessler; "tell me all about it."

And he patted Friesshardt on the head. Friesshardt bellowed.

Gessler beckoned to one of his courtiers.

"Have you a handkerchief?" he said.

"I have a handkerchief, your Excellency."

"Then dry this man's eyes."

The courtier did as he was bidden.

"*Now*," said Gessler, when the drying was done, and Friesshardt's tears had ceased, "what has been happening here? I heard a cry of 'Help!' as I came up. Who cried 'Help!'?"

"Please, your lordship's noble Excellencyship," said Friesshardt, "it was me, Friesshardt."

"You should say, 'It was I,' " said Gessler. "Proceed."

"Which I am a loyal servant of your Excellency's, and in your Excellency's army, and seeing as how I was told to stand by this 'ere pole and guard that there hat, I stood by this 'ere pole, and guarded that there hat—all day, I did, your Excellency. And then up comes this man here, and I says to him—'Bow down to the hat,' I says. 'Ho!' he says to me—'ho, indeed!' and he passed on without so much as nodding. So I takes my pike, and I taps him on the head to remind him, as you may say, that there was something he was forgetting, and he ups and hits me, he does. And then the crowd runs up with their sticks and hits me and Leuthold cruel, your Excellency. And while we was a-fighting with them, this here man I'm a-telling you about, your Excellency, he outs with an arrow, puts it into his bow, and sends it through the hat, and I don't see how you'll ever be able to wear it again. It's a waste of a good hat, your Excellency—that's what it is. And then the people, they puts me and Leuthold on the ground, and hoists this here man—Tell, they call him—up on their shoulders, and he starts making a speech, when up you comes, your Excellency. That's how it all was."

Gessler turned pale with rage, and glared fiercely at Tell, who stood before him in the grasp of two of the bodyguard.

"Ah," he said, "Tell, is it? Good-day to you, Tell. I think we've met before, Tell? Eh, Tell?"

"We have, your Excellency. It was in the ravine of Schächenthal," said Tell firmly.

"Your memory is good, Tell. So is mine. I think you made a few remarks to me on that occasion, Tell—a few chatty remarks? Eh, Tell?"

"Very possibly, your Excellency."

"You were hardly polite, Tell."

"If I offended you I am sorry."

"I am glad to hear it, Tell. I think you will be even sorrier before long. So you've been ill-treating my soldiers, eh?"

"It was not I who touched them."

"Oh, so you didn't touch them? Ah! But you defied my power by refusing to bow down to the hat. I set up that hat to prove the people's loyalty. I am afraid you are not loyal, Tell."

"I was a little thoughtless, not disloyal. I passed the hat without thinking."

"You should always think, Tell. It is very dangerous not to do so. And I suppose that you shot your arrow through the hat without thinking?"

"I was a little carried away by excitement, your Excellency."

"Dear, dear! Carried away by excitement, were you? You must really be more careful, Tell. One of these days you will be getting yourself into trouble. But it seems to have been a very fine shot. You *are* a capital marksman, I believe?"

"Father's the best shot in all Switzerland," piped a youthful voice. "He can hit an apple on a tree a hundred yards away. I've seen him. Can't you, father?"

Walter, who had run away when the fighting began, had returned on seeing his father in the hands of the soldiers.

Gessler turned a cold eye upon him.

"Who is this?" he asked.

## Chapter 11

It is my son Walter, your Excellency," said Tell.

"Your son? Indeed. This is very interesting. Have you any more children?"

"I have one other boy."

"And which of them do you love the most, eh?"

"I love them both alike, your Excellency."

"Dear me! Quite a happy family. Now, listen to me, Tell. I know you are fond of excitement, so I am going to try to give you a little. Your son says that you can hit an apple on a tree a hundred yards away, and I am sure you have every right to be very proud of such a feat. Friesshardt!"

"Your Excellency?"

"Bring me an apple."

Friesshardt picked one up. Some apples had been thrown at him and Leuthold earlier in the day, and there were several lying about.

"Which I'm afraid as how it's a little bruised, your Excellency," he said, "having hit me on the helmet."

"Thank you. I do not require it for eating purposes," said Gessler. "Now, Tell, I have here an apple—a simple apple, not overripe. I should like to test that feat of yours. So take your bow—I see you have it in your hand—and get ready to shoot. I am going to put this apple on your son's head. He will be placed a hundred yards away from you, and if you do not hit the apple with your first shot your life shall pay forfeit."

And he regarded Tell with a look of malicious triumph.

"Your Excellency, it cannot be!" cried Tell, "the thing is

too monstrous. Perhaps your Excellency is pleased to jest. You cannot bid a father shoot an apple from off his son's head! Consider, your Excellency!"

"You shall shoot the apple from off the head of this boy," said Gessler sternly. "I do not jest. That is my will."

"Sooner would I die," said Tell.

"If you do not shoot you die with the boy. Come, come, Tell, why so cautious? They always told me that you loved perilous enterprises, and yet when I give you one you complain. I could understand anybody else shrinking from the feat. But you! Hitting apples at a hundred yards is child's play to you. And what does it matter where the apple is— whether it is on a tree or on a boy's head? It is an apple just the same. Proceed, Tell."

The crowd, seeing a discussion going on, had left the edge of the meadow and clustered round to listen. A groan of dismay went up at the Governor's words.

"Down on your knees, boy," whispered Rudolph der Harras to Walter—"down on your knees, and beg his Excellency for your life."

"I won't!" said Walter stoutly.

"Come," said Gessler, "clear a path there—clear a path! Hurry yourselves. I won't have this loitering. Look you, Tell: Attend to me for a moment. I find you in the middle of this meadow deliberately defying my authority and making sport of my orders. I find you in the act of stirring up discontent among my people with speeches. I might have you executed without ceremony. But do I? No. Nobody shall say that Hermann Gessler the Governor is not kind-hearted. I say to myself, 'I will give this man one chance.' I place your fate in your own skillful hands. How can a man complain of harsh treatment when he is made master of his own fate? Besides, I don't ask you to do anything difficult. I merely bid you perform what must be to you a simple shot. You boast of your unerring aim. Now is the time to prove it. Clear the way there!"

Walter Fürst flung himself on his knees before the Governor.

"Your Highness," he cried, "none deny your power. Let it be mingled with mercy. It is excellent, as an English poet will say in a few hundred years, to have a giant's strength, but it is tyrannous to use it like a giant. Take the half of my possessions, but spare my son-in-law."

But Walter Tell broke in impatiently, and bade his grandfather rise, and not kneel to the tyrant.

"Where must I stand?" asked he. "I'm not afraid. Father can hit a bird upon the wing."

"You see that lime tree yonder," said Gessler to his soldiers, "take the boy and bind him to it."

"I will not be bound!" cried Walter. "I am not afraid. I'll stand still. I won't breathe. If you bind me I'll kick!"

"Let us bind your eyes, at least," said Rudolph der Harras.

"Do you think I fear to see father shoot?" said Walter. "I won't stir an eyelash. Father, show the tyrant how you can shoot. He thinks you're going to miss. Isn't he an old donkey!"

"Very well, young man," muttered Gessler, "we'll see who is laughing five minutes from now." And once more he bade the crowd stand back and leave a way clear for Tell to shoot.

# *Chapter 12*

The crowd fell back, leaving a lane down which Walter walked, carrying the apple. There was dead silence as he passed. Then the people began to whisper excitedly to one another.

"Shall this be done before our eyes?" said Arnold of Melchthal to Werner Stauffacher. "Of what use was it that we swore an oath to rebel if we permit this? Let us rise and slay the tyrant."

Werner Stauffacher, prudent man, scratched his chin thoughtfully.

"We-e-ll," he said, "you see, the difficulty is that we are not armed and the soldiers *are*. There is nothing I should enjoy more than slaying the tyrant, only I have an idea that the tyrant would slay us. You see my point?"

"Why were we so slow!" groaned Arnold. "We should have risen before, and then this would never have happened. Who was it that advised us to delay?"

"We-e-ll," said Stauffacher (who had himself advised delay), "I can't quite remember at the moment, but I dare say you could find out by looking up the minutes of our last meeting. I know the motion was carried by a majority of two votes. See! Gessler grows impatient."

Gessler, who had been fidgeting on his horse for some time, now spoke again, urging Tell to hurry.

"Begin!" he cried—"begin!"

"Immediately," replied Tell, fitting the arrow to the string.

Gessler began to mock him once more.

"You see now," he said, "the danger of carrying arms. I don't know if you have ever noticed it, but arrows very often recoil on the man who carries them. The only man who has any business to possess a weapon is the ruler of a country—myself, for instance. A low, common fellow—if you will excuse the description—like yourself only grows proud through being armed, and so offends those above him. But, of course, it's no business of mine. I am only telling you what I think about it. Personally, I like to encourage my subjects to shoot; that is why I am giving you such a splendid mark to shoot at. You see, Tell?"

Tell did not reply. He raised his bow and pointed it.

There was a stir of excitement in the crowd, more particularly in that part of the crowd which stood on his right, for, his hand trembling for the first time in his life, Tell had pointed his arrow, not at his son, but straight into the heart of the crowd.

"Here! Hi! That's the wrong way! More to the left!" shouted the people in a panic, while Gessler roared with laughter, and bade Tell shoot and chance it.

"If you can't hit the apple or your son," he chuckled, "you can bring down one of your dear fellow-countrymen."

Tell lowered his bow, and a sigh of relief went through the crowd.

"My eyes are swimming," he said, "I cannot see."

Then he turned to the Governor.

"I cannot shoot," he said, "bid your soldiers kill me."

"No," said Gessler—"no, Tell. That is not at all what I want. If I had wished my soldiers to kill you, I should not have waited for a formal invitation from you. I have no desire to see you slain. Not at present. I wish to see you shoot. Come, Tell, they say you can do everything, and are afraid of nothing. Only the other day, I hear, you carried a man, one Baumgartner—that was his name, I think—across a rough sea in an open boat. You may remember it? I particularly wished to catch Baumgartner, Tell. Now, this is a feat which calls for much less courage. Simply to shoot an apple off a boy's head. A child could do it."

While he was speaking, Tell had been standing in silence, his hands trembling and his eyes fixed, sometimes on the Governor, sometimes on the sky. He now seized his quiver, and taking from it a second arrow, placed it in his belt. Gessler watched him, but said nothing.

"Shoot, father!" cried Walter from the other end of the lane, "I'm not afraid."

Tell, calm again now, raised his bow and took a steady aim. Everybody craned forward, the front ranks in vain telling those behind that there was nothing to be gained by pushing. Gessler bent over his horse's neck and peered eagerly towards Walter. A great hush fell on all as Tell released the string.

"Phut!" went the string, and the arrow rushed through the air.

A moment's suspense, and then a terrific cheer rose from the spectators.

The apple had leaped from Walter's head, pierced through the center.

## *Chapter 13*

Intense excitement instantly reigned. Their suspense over, the crowd cheered again and again, shook hands with one another, and flung their caps into the air. Everyone was delighted, for everyone was fond of Tell and Walter. It also pleased them to see the Governor disappointed. He had had things his own way for so long that it was a pleasant change to see him baffled in this manner. Not since Switzerland became a nation had the meadow outside the city gates been the scene of such rejoicings.

Walter had picked up the apple with the arrow piercing it, and was showing it proudly to all his friends.

"I told you so," he kept saying; "I knew father wouldn't hurt me. Father's the best shot in all Switzerland."

"That was indeed a shot!" exclaimed Ulric the smith; "it will ring through the ages. While the mountains stand will the tale of Tell the bowman be told."

Rudolph der Harras took the apple from Walter and showed it to Gessler, who had been sitting transfixed on his horse.

"See," he said, "the arrow has passed through the very center. It was a master shot."

"It was very nearly a 'Master Walter shot,'" said Rösselmann the priest severely, fixing the Governor with a stern eye.

Gessler made no answer. He sat looking moodily at Tell, who had dropped his crossbow and was standing motionless, still gazing in the direction in which the arrow had sped. Nobody liked to be the first to speak to him.

"Well," said Rudolph der Harras, breaking an awkward silence, "I suppose it's all over now? May as well be moving, eh?"

He bit a large piece out of the apple, which he still held. Walter uttered a piercing scream as he saw the mouthful disappear. Up till now he had shown no signs of dismay, in spite of the peril which he had had to face; but when he watched Rudolph eating the apple, which he naturally looked upon as his own property, he could not keep quiet any longer. Rudolph handed him the apple with an apology, and he began to munch it contentedly.

"Come with me to your mother, my boy," said Rösselmann.

Walter took no notice, but went on eating the apple.

Tell came to himself with a start, looked round for Walter, and began to lead him away in the direction of his home, deaf to all the cheering that was going on around him.

Gessler leaned forward in his saddle.

"Tell," he said, "a word with you."

Tell came back.

"Your Excellency?"

"Before you go I wish you to explain one thing."

"A thousand, your Excellency."

"No, only one. When you were getting ready to shoot at the apple you placed an arrow in the string and a second arrow in your belt."

"A second arrow!" Tell pretended to be very much astonished, but the pretence did not deceive the Governor.

"Yes, a second arrow. Why was that? What did you intend to do with that arrow, Tell?"

Tell looked down uneasily, and twisted his bow about in his hands.

"My lord," he said at last, "it is a bowman's custom. All archers place a second arrow in their belt."

"No, Tell," said Gessler, "I cannot take that answer as the truth. 1 know there was some other meaning in what you did. Tell me the reason without concealment. Why was it? Your life is safe, whatever it was, so speak out. Why did you take out that second arrow?"

Tell stopped fidgeting with his bow, and met the Governor's eye with a steady gaze.

"Since you promise me my life, your Excellency," he replied, drawing himself up, "I will tell you."

He drew the arrow from his belt and held it up.

The crowd pressed forward, hanging on his words.

"Had my first arrow," said Tell slowly, "pierced my child and not the apple, this would have pierced you, my lord. Had I missed with my first shot, be sure, my lord, that my second would have found its mark."

A murmur of approval broke from the crowd as Tell thrust the arrow back into the quiver and faced the Governor with folded arms and burning eyes. Gessler turned white with fury.

"Seize that man!" he shouted.

"My lord, bethink you," whispered Rudolph der Harras; "you promised him his life. Tell, fly!" he cried.

Tell did not move.

"Seize that man and bind him," roared Gessler once more. "If he resists, cut him down."

"I shall not resist," said Tell scornfully. "I should have known the folly of trusting to a tyrant to keep his word. My death will at least show my countrymen the worth of their Governor's promises."

"Not so," replied Gessler; "no man shall say I ever broke my knightly word. I promised you your life, and I will give you your life. But you are a dangerous man, Tell, and against such must I guard myself. You have told me your murderous purpose. I must look to it that that purpose is not fulfilled. Life I promised you, and life I will give you. But of freedom I said nothing. In my castle at Küssnacht there are dungeons where no ray of sun or moon ever falls. Chained hand and foot in one of these, you will hardly aim your arrows at me. It is rash, Tell, to threaten those who have power over you. Soldiers, bind him and lead him to my ship. I will follow, and will myself conduct him to Küssnacht."

The soldiers tied Tell's hands. He offered no resistance. And amidst the groans of the people he was led away to the shore of the lake, where Gessler's ship lay at anchor.

"Our last chance is gone," said the people to one another. "Where shall we look now for a leader?"

## Chapter 14

The castle of Küssnacht lay on the opposite side of the lake, a mighty mass of stone reared on a mightier crag rising sheer out of the waves which boiled and foamed about its foot. Steep rocks of fantastic shape hemmed it in, and many were the vessels which perished on these, driven thither by the frequent storms that swept over the lake.

Gessler and his men, Tell in their midst, bound and unarmed, embarked early in the afternoon at Flüelen, which was the name of the harbor where the Governor's ship had been moored. Flüelen was about two miles from Küssnacht.

When they had arrived at the vessel they went on board, and Tell was placed at the bottom of the hold. It was pitch dark, and rats scampered over his body as he lay. The ropes were cast off, the sails filled, and the ship made her way across the lake, aided by a favoring breeze.

A large number of the Swiss people had followed Tell and his captors to the harbor, and stood gazing sorrowfully after the ship as it diminished in the distance. There had been whispers of an attempted rescue, but nobody had dared to begin it, and the whispers had led to nothing. Few of the people carried weapons, and the soldiers were clad in armor, and each bore a long pike or a sharp sword. As Arnold of Sewa would have said if he had been present, what the people wanted was prudence. It was useless to attack men so thoroughly able to defend themselves.

Therefore the people looked on and groaned, but did nothing.

For some time the ship sped easily on her way and through a calm sea. Tell lay below, listening to the trampling of the sailors overhead, as they ran about the deck, and gave up all hope of ever seeing his home and his friends again.

But soon he began to notice that the ship was rolling and pitching more than it had been doing at first, and it was not long before he realized that a very violent storm had begun. Storms sprung up very suddenly on the lake, and made it unsafe for boats that attempted to cross it. Often the sea was quite unruffled at the beginning of the crossing, and was rough enough at the end to wreck the largest ship.

Tell welcomed the storm. He had no wish to live if life meant years of imprisonment in a dark dungeon of Castle Küssnacht. Drowning would be a pleasant fate compared with that. He lay at the bottom of the ship, hoping that the next wave would dash them on to a rock and send them to the bottom of the lake. The tossing became worse and worse.

Upon the deck Gessler was standing beside the helmsman, and gazing anxiously across the waters at the rocks that fringed the narrow entrance to the bay a few hundred yards

to the east of Castle Küssnacht. This bay was the only spot
for miles along the shore at which it was possible to land
safely. For miles on either side the coast was studded with
great rocks, which would have dashed a ship to pieces in a
moment. It was to this bay that Gessler wished to direct the
ship. But the helmsman told him that he could not make
sure of finding the entrance, so great was the cloud of spray
which covered it. A mistake would mean shipwreck.

"My lord," said the helmsman, "I have neither strength
nor skill to guide the helm. I do not know which way to
turn."

"What are we to do?" asked Rudolph der Harras, who was
standing near.

The helmsman hesitated. Then he spoke, eyeing the Governor uneasily.

"Tell could steer us through," he said, "if your lordship
would but give him the helm."

Gessler started.

"Tell!" he muttered. "Tell!"

The ship drew nearer to the rocks.

"Bring him here," said Gessler.

Two soldiers went down to the hold and released Tell.
They bade him get up and come with them. Tell followed
them on deck, and stood before the Governor.

"Tell," said Gessler.

Tell looked at him without speaking.

"Take the helm, Tell," said Gessler, "and steer the ship
through those rocks into the bay beyond, or instant death
shall be your lot."

Without a word Tell took the helmsman's place, peering
keenly into the cloud of foam before him. To right and to
left he turned the vessel's head, and to right again, into the
very heart of the spray. They were right among the rocks
now, but the ship did not strike on them. Quivering and
pitching, she was hurried along, until of a sudden the spray

cloud was behind her, and in front the calm waters of the bay.

Gessler beckoned to the helmsman.

"Take the helm again," he said.

He pointed to Tell.

"Bind him," he said to the soldiers.

The soldiers advanced slowly, for they were loath to bind the man who had just saved them from destruction. But the Governor's orders must be obeyed, so they came towards Tell, carrying ropes with which to bind him.

Tell moved a step back. The ship was gliding past a lofty rock. It was such a rock as Tell had often climbed when hunting the chamois. He acted with the quickness of the hunter. Snatching up the bow and quiver which lay on the deck, he sprang on to the bulwark of the vessel, and, with a mighty leap, gained the rock. Another instant, and he was out of reach.

Gessler roared to his bowmen.

"Shoot! shoot!!" he cried.

The bowmen hastily fitted arrow to string. They were too late. Tell was ready before them. There was a hiss as the shaft rushed through the air, and the next moment Gessler the Governor fell dead on the deck, pierced through the heart.

Tell's second arrow had found its mark, as his first had done.

# Chapter 15

There is not much more of the story of William Tell. The death of Gessler was a signal to the Swiss to rise in revolt, and soon the whole country was up in arms against the Austrians. It had been chiefly the fear of the Governor that had prevented a rising before. It had been brewing for a long time. The people had been bound by a solemn oath to drive the enemy out of the country. All through Switzerland preparations for a revolution were going on, and nobles and peasants had united.

Directly the news arrived that the Governor was slain, meetings of the people were held in every town in Switzerland, and it was resolved to begin the revolution without delay. All the fortresses that Gessler had built during his years of rule were carried by assault on the same night. The last to fall was one which had only been begun a short time back, and the people who had been forced to help to build it spent a very pleasant hour pulling down the stones which had cost them such labor to put in their place. Even the children helped. It was a great treat to them to break what they pleased without being told not to.

"See," said Tell, as he watched them, "in years to come, when these same children are gray-haired, they will remember this night as freshly as they will remember it tomorrow."

A number of people rushed up, bearing the pole which Gessler's soldiers had set up in the meadow. The hat was still on top of it, nailed to the wood by Tell's arrow.

"Here's the hat!" shouted Ruodi—"the hat to which we were to bow!"

"What shall we do with it?" cried several voices.

"Destroy it! Burn it!" said others. "To the flames with this emblem of tyranny!"

But Tell stopped them.

"Let us preserve it," he said. "Gessler set it up to be a means of enslaving the country; we will set it up as a memorial of our newly-gained liberty. Nobly is fulfilled the oath we swore to drive the tyrants from our land. Let the pole mark the spot where the revolution finished."

"But *is* it finished?" said Arnold of Melchthal. "It is a nice point. When the Emperor of Austria hears that we have killed his friend Gessler, and burnt down all his fine new fortresses, will he not come here to seek revenge?"

"He will," said Tell. "And let him come. And let him bring all his mighty armies. We have driven out the enemy that was in our land. We will meet and drive away the enemy that comes from another country. Switzerland is not easy to attack. There are but a few mountain passes by which the foe can approach. We will stop these with our bodies. And one great strength we have: we are united. And united we need fear no foe."

"Hurrah!" shouted everybody.

"But who is this that approaches?" said Tell. "He seems excited. Perhaps he brings news."

It was Rösselmann the pastor, and he brought stirring news.

"These are strange times in which we live," said Rösselmann, coming up.

'Why, what has happened?" cried everybody.

"Listen, and be amazed."

"Why, what's the matter?"

"The Emperor——"

"Yes?"

"The Emperor is dead."

"What! dead?"

"Dead!"

"Impossible! How came you by the news?"

"John Müller of Schaffhausen brought it. And he is a truthful man."

"But how did it happen?"

"As the Emperor rode from Stein to Baden the lords of Eschenbach and Tegerfelden, jealous, it is said, of his power, fell upon him with their spears. His bodyguard were on the other side of a stream—the Emperor had just crossed it—and could not come to his assistance. He died instantly."

By the death of the Emperor the revolution in Switzerland was enabled to proceed without check. The successor of the Emperor had too much to do in defending himself against the slayers of his father to think of attacking the Swiss, and by the time he was at leisure they were too strong to be attacked. So the Swiss became free.

As for William Tell, he retired to his home, and lived there very happily ever afterwards with his wife and his two sons, who in a few years became very nearly as skillful in the use of the crossbow as their father.

## *Epilogue*

Some say the tale related here
Is amplified and twisted;
Some say it isn't very clear
That William Tell existed;
Some say he freed his country *so,*
The Governor demolished.
Perhaps he did. I only know
That taxes aren't abolished!